STORM TO STILLNESS

THE CALM THAT WE CARRY

Yuvaan
books
An Imprint of Unbound Script

Storm to Stillness

Written *by* Shweta Padda

ISBN : 978-93-47125-77-5

First Edition : January, 2026

Publisher : Unbound Script
2/41, Ansari Road
Daryaganj, Delhi-110002
Website : www.unboundscript.com
E-mail : books@unboundscript.com
Phone : 011-35807601

Printer : Vikas Computer & Printers, Ghaziaba, U.P.d

Price : ₹ 249/-

STORM TO STILLNESS

THE CALM THAT WE CARRY

Shweta Padda

Yuvaan
books

CONTENTS

DEDICATION

To my sons, Jishan and Sharaj– my spine, my strength, my reason through every storm.

To my parents, who gave me the courage, discipline, and home.

To Jiya, Vineeta, and Akshat Gupta ji, my mentor who guided me in this journey.

And above all, to Maa Lalita Tripura Sundari– this book is written in silence, courage and love.

PROLOGUE

We usually unlock our phones the moment we wake up, before our eyes are fully open–thumb hunting for an email badge or a glowing red notification that promised urgency but delivered almost nothing. By noon, that screen will have lit up in our hands another sixty or seventy times. Strangely, the more it buzzes, the emptier the day can feel, as though each vibration scrapes away a slice of attention we meant to spend on something that mattered.

I know this storm well. I once found myself scrolling news headlines at a traffic light, convinced I was "multitasking," when really, I was just afraid of the quiet that settles in when the world isn't jerking the leash of my mind.

This book is not an escape from modern life. It is an invitation, a shared experiment in learning how to enter that quiet without abandoning the lives we've built. I am not here to sell you a cabin in the woods, a juice cleanse, or a vow of silence. I am here to show you that stillness can be woven into commutes, deadlines, group chats, ambitions, and even Netflix queues.

The promise is simple:

When we learn to be calm at the center of our own whirlwind, life stops feeling like something that is happening to us and starts feeling like something we are consciously shaping, one breath at a time.

Why does this matter now?

Because the pace of the world has outrun the wiring of our nervous systems. Ancient sages warned us about the "monkey mind," but they never had to answer Slack pings at midnight or measure self-worth in hearts and thumbs. Neuroscience keeps confirming what the Upanishads hinted at long ago: an untamed mind loops in fear, scarcity, and comparison. The result is a cultural form of spiritual jet lag– we move faster than our souls can travel, and we end up both exhausted and strangely absent from our own lives.

Close that gap, and energy, clarity, even delight begin to seep back in.

Over the years, I began to see the same hunger everywhere– including in myself. We want the depth promised by spiritual traditions, but in language that doesn't require trading reason for incense. So instead of preaching, I collected stories and distilled practices that are ancient in spirit, modern in form, and practical by design.

Five threads run through every chapter:

Stillness: not as a luxury, but as a daily muscle we can exercise in three-minute intervals while the chai drips.

Presence: the art of actually inhabiting the moment we're in.

Surrender: not weakness, but the ultimate power that makes us realise control was nothing but an illusion.

Connection: because inner peace is not only an inside job; we co-regulate, heal, and grow in a relationship.

Ritual: small, repeatable acts that remind the nervous system where home is, even when the world feels like a Category-5 storm.

If you're holding this book, there's a good chance you've already felt the cost of constant motion. Maybe you're a parent watching evenings dissolve into the blue glow of devices. Maybe you're a professional haunted by the whisper, Is this it? Or you're a student feeling the pressure of AI-curves and the sucking undertow of comparisons. Whoever you are, you are not here for abstract enlightenment. You are here because you need tools that fit inside real life.

Here is what you will take away:

- a five-minute practice that interrupts overthinking before it snowballs into insomnia;
- a morning ritual that makes waking intentional instead of accidental;

- experiments with digital fasting that reclaim dopamine without wrecking careers;
- a surrender journal that converts worry into trust, one scribbled line at a time.

These micro-habits stitch together, and one day you may notice something almost embarrassing in its simplicity, the peace you thought required a sabbatical was hiding in plain sight beneath the noise of striving.

Along the way you'll meet personal stories, scientific snapshots, poetry, scripture, and confession. On one page you will find me quoting Gita while on the next I'd be seen admitting that I once tried to meditate with my smartwatch on, until a meeting reminder shattered the mood and taught me more about ego than any scripture ever could. You'll be asked questions, some playful and some uncomfortable, because inquiry is the doorway to awareness, and awareness is the soil where stillness takes root.

Think of each chapter as a long conversation over masala chai, the kind where time disappears because the talk is real and neither of us checks our phone.

Does this guarantee a life without storms?

Of course not. Storms are part of being human.

What changes is our relationship with the thunder.

Instead of being flung around by every gust, we learn to stand at the eye– observing, responding, stepping forward with purpose. From there, anxiety becomes information, busyness becomes choice, and even grief becomes a teacher instead of a jailer.

This is not a quick fix. There is no overnight shipping for transcendence. But if you engage the reflections, try the practices, and allow yourself to be surprised, subtle shifts accumulate. One morning you'll notice your jaw isn't clenched in traffic. One conversation will feel richer because you are actually listening. Slowly, an inner spaciousness emerges that no amount of multitasking could ever create.

In the end, this book is a love letter to your attention.
Where it goes, your life goes.
Where it rests, your power grows.

So take a slow breath right now. Feel the weight of the page in your hand. Notice the gentle pulse in your fingertips.

That tiny flicker of awareness is proof: The journey has already begun.

Turn the page.

Let's step into the eye of the storm: still, steady, and fully alive.

Chapter 1

The Ancient Whisper: Why We're Restless

The Murmur Beneath the Noise

If we close our eyes for a moment and simply listen, we'll notice two kinds of sounds. One is the clear, exterior clamour–traffic sliding past the curb, a fridge motor humming, maybe our neighbour's music seeping through a wall. And then there's an understated soundtrack just underneath, an almost inaudible murmur that feels older than all the rest. It is a steady throb of thoughts arriving uninvited, a churning of desires and doubts, memories replaying their greatest hits, and an itch to do something–anything–other than to remain still.

You know, the first time I truly noticed that inner murmur, I was standing in the middle of the Square, of all places. Digital screens flickered in every direction. Cabs, cars, buses prowled. Tourists stood pointing upward, mouths open. I had travelled out on my day off, armed with my diary and a pen. Yet the loudest thing in that intersection was not the horns or the advertisements, but the thought-spiral in my own head.

Did I turn off the gas stove at home? Why did that one email from my creative director sound so abrupt? Should I record a video or take some photos for my Instagram account? What if I miss the perfect caption and– having lost around 35k followers just in a week– only end up feeling more embarrassed?

My mind, like everyone else's, was drumming its anxious fingers on the table.

That whirlpool followed me back to the hotel and even into sleep. The next morning, scrolling through the photos I had taken, I noticed something odd. Every snapshot of the Square showed at least a dozen faces staring not at the billboards but at the rectangles glowing in their palms. It dawned on me that the Square, that metaphor for modern frenzy, had been relocated into each person's pocket. The real storm was inside us.

Yet the whisper pre-dates pixels and push notifications. Long before skyscrapers and silicon chips, ancient mystics squinted inward and heard the same turbulence.

They gave it a name–*in the Indian Upanishads, the chitta-vrtti, the mind-stuff forever swirling; in early Buddhist texts, the restlessness of the monkey mind; in Greek philosophy, the peripatetic logos that refuse to sit still. They called the external world* **māyā**, *a shimmering curtain, precisely because they recognised an internal projector that keeps flicking stories onto the screen.*

Why are we, the twenty-first-century wanderers, still restless even after all our comfort upgrades? Why do we, with ergonomic chairs and noise-cancelling headphones, feel more fidgety than the hunter-gatherers who slept on moss?

This chapter is an excavation. We will try to brush away the dust of centuries to rediscover the ancient whisper, then shine the flashlight of neuroscience on it, and finally test both against our own direct experience. My promise is not to silence the murmur, but we'll soon see that silence is not achieved by wrestling sound to the ground. It's realised when we hear it for what it truly is: an invitation hidden beneath agitation.

Don't forget I am just sharing my own experience journey.

A Mind Older Than Our Smartphones

The year my niece turned three, she liked to play a game called "Why." We might be familiar with it. I would tell her, "Time to put on our shoes," and she'd ask, "Why?" I'd reply, "Because we're going outside." "Why?" "Because fresh air is good." "Why?" The cascade would continue until either I surrendered or she discovered a more exciting distraction, like the neighbour's dog.

The human mind has not grown out of that phase. Why is the grass moving? Why does my stomach hurt? Why did the fruit taste bitter? That probing instinct kept our ancestors alive. Those who ignored the rustle in the grass became lunch- those who investigated lived long enough to pass on their genes for vigilance. We are the great-great-great-grandchildren of professional "worriers".

Yet nature crafted us for episodic bursts of alertness, not for a permanent, caffeinated state. A leopard spotted on the horizon induced a spike in cortisol and adrenaline, muscles braced, senses sharpened. When the danger passed, chemistry subsided- the tribe returned to laughing around the fire, telling stories about the near miss. Today, the leopard has donned Wi-Fi and corporate logos. It pings us at odd hours, tracks our gaze, measures our performance metrics, sends a late-night Slack that starts with "Quick question-." The body still reacts with the same ancient alarms, only the off-switch is hard to find.

Evolutionary psychologists call this mismatch *the stone-age brain in the silicon-age world.* Our hardware was coded for scarcity, sudden peril, and short bursts of effort. Our software–the apps, notifications, and endless content loops–exploits those reflexes, promising novelty and belonging, while rarely delivering the real nutrient: the deep, sustained connection. As a result, we can spend an evening browsing the highlight reels of other people's lives, absorbing information faster than any previous human, and yet feel starved for meaning by bedtime.

The Monkey and The Mirage

Buddhists used a vivid metaphor- the mind is like a monkey, drunk and swinging from branch to branch, chattering and shrieking. The image is almost comical until we try to meditate for five minutes and realize the old sages weren't exaggerating. My first silent retreat [The Art of Living] confirmed this. I'd imagined that silence would be like a spa for the soul–scented candles and effortless calm. Instead, sitting cross-legged, I discovered a primate circus inside my skull. One minute I was replaying high-school embarrassments, and the next minute I was planning dinner.

This monkey is restless enough as it is and the Upanishads add yet another layer of trickery. In simpler terms: our minds are constantly agitated and overloaded, and the subtle insights of the Upanishads often make the inner landscape feel even more intricate and difficult to settle into clarity, rather than calming them immediately.

And that is when they describe the world as "maya", often translated as "illusion." Modern readers sometimes dismiss this as escapist mysticism, but maya does not mean that the material world is fake, it means our perception is filtered through projections, desires, and fears. Suppose a friend isn't replying to our message. Within an hour, our mind generates twenty different interpretations– he must be angry, maybe I said something wrong, perhaps her phone battery died, or the worst, they met with an accident. The mind paints a cinematic plotline on the blank canvas of silence, and then reacts emotionally to its own creation. *That self-spun story is maya in action.*

Combine this drunk monkey with maya's projectors, and we get a restless empire whose borders extend into every corner of our everyday life. We pace from the kitchen to the living room, swinging the refrigerator door, not because we're hungry but because this mind is allergic to stillness. We watch the news, telling ourselves how we need to be informed, but find the headlines stoke fear rather than wisdom.

Ancient sages were keen psychologists. They didn't own MRI machines, yet mapped the same terrain the neuroscientists are charting now. They observed that chasing the monkey through the jungle only makes him swing faster. They also discovered that we can't shut down a hallucination– we have to see through it. Stillness, they taught, is less about slamming the brakes and more about stepping back and watching the engine run by itself. Instead of diving in and grabbing each wave, it's about sitting by the bank of the river while the water rushes past.

When Science Meets Scriptures

Modern neuroscience has entered the conversation waving colourful brain scans. Functional MRI studies reveal that the mind's Default Mode Network, often abbreviated as DMN, kicks in when we are not focused on an external task. The DMN is responsible for daydreaming, self-referential thinking, rumination, mind-wandering, social cognition and the spool of inner chatter. It is, in effect, the biological stage on which our monkey swings.

What fascinates me is how closely the DMN's activity mirrors ancient diagnoses of mental suffering. Excessive activation correlates with anxiety disorders, depression, and even attention deficits. The Upanishads asserted that untrained mind-stuff generates 'dukha' or suffering; the Buddha described craving and aversion as the root of disease, modern clinicians note that over-identification with mental narratives fuels stress and burnout.

Equally striking is what happens when practices like meditation, chanting, or slow breathing enter the scene. Researchers observed that Tibetan monks in deep meditation had their DMN activity quietened dramatically, while regions governing the present-moment awareness lit up. The same effects, albeit less pronounced, occur in beginners after just eight weeks of mindfulness training. Brain waves shift into alpha and theta ranges, associated with relaxed but alert consciousness. The science is not mystical proof but a dialogue– the monks say, "Sit still, breathe, watch thoughts pass like clouds." The machine replies, "Roger that, the chatter circuit dims."

Skeptics might argue that meditation merely calms the brain in the way a sleeping pill induces drowsiness. Yet experienced practitioners report heightened clarity, not dullness. Imagine, for example, a lake whose surface has been whipped by the wind. Sunlight scatters, and we cannot see the fish below. Still the air, and the water clears– the fish do not cease to exist, we simply perceive them. In the same way, stillness reveals rather than anaesthetises. When we are still– mentally and emotionally– we do not shut down or escape reality; instead, we become more aware and perceptive.

A Train Ride Into Silence

One might think, "Well, these sages and monks have time to stare at walls– I have deadlines to meet."

Let's understand this with a real-life example. A friend of mine, Sharaj, works as a UX designer at a startup famous for its motto– Move fast and don't break things, just repeat them. He absorbs metrics like breaths– activation rates, churns, engagement. One October morning, commuting from Pune to Mumbai, his phone battery died a sudden, merciless death. He didn't have a portable charger, and all the charging outlets in the train were occupied. Panic surged first. No calendar, no email sneak peeks, no Spotify. His hands lay uselessly in his lap.

Two or three stations later, an odd sensation rose– equal parts nostalgia and novelty. He could hear the rhythmic click of wheels against track, once so familiar in childhood before streaming headphones occupied travel. He noticed an elderly man reading "The Naga Warriors" by Akshat Gupta, a national best selling author, turning pages with deliberate relish. Then he saw a teenage couple, laughing over a single pastry, completely absorbed into each other. A slant of sunlight carved through the window, dust motes twirling like tiny planets.

"Time expanded," he told me later. "But more than that, I expanded. Instead of living inside the phone, for once, I was living inside the moment." By the time the train rolled into Dadar Station, he felt rested in a way that eight hours of sleep hadn't delivered in a long time. He recognised how addicted he had been to constant stimulation.

The real epiphany came that evening. Sorting through his to-do list, Sharaj realised his mind kept returning to the peaceful tune of the train ride. He decided to replicate the experiment. Every day on his commute, the phone stayed in his laptop bag. Soon, he began noticing micro-details he'd missed for years: wall paintings, patterns morphing along the track walls, the station announcements, and even the subtle weather shifts over the river. The external world hadn't changed– his attention had.

A month later, he added a five-minute sitting practice before bed. Nothing fancy, just closing his eyes, following the breath, and watching thoughts float by. He reported fewer anxiety spikes, a decrease in compulsive email checking, and a humorous distance from his own dramas. "The monkey still chatters," he said, "but I don't surrender the keys anymore."

Sitting With the Echo

The sages would applaud Sharaj. They knew that stillness is portable, and that small windows of silence can introduce us to a hall of mirrors where we finally meet our own reflection beyond roles and avatars.

Rumi writes, "There is a voice that doesn't use words. Listen."

Each points to the same discovery– underneath the roar of existence lies a quiet seat from which we can witness the play.

We don't have to retreat to a Himalayan cave. We can begin where we are. Next time you stand in a grocery line, resist the reflex to refresh notifications. *Allow boredom–it is fertile soil.*

Watch how quickly our mind hunts for hooks. Name the thoughts softly–planning, worrying, remembering, fantasising. As we label them, their grip loosens. This is not repression but recognition. The monkey, caught mid-swing, begins to tire when we shine a light on his antics.

Over weeks, a pattern unfolds. The same few thoughts repeat like a greatest-hits album. I'm not good enough. What if they reject me? If only I had more money, time, and love. Seeing the loop is the first revolution–we realise novelty is largely recycled content dressed in new costumes. The Upanishads compare the human mind to a weaver spinning endless cloth from a single thread of awareness. Notice the weave and we reclaim the loom.

My own practice started with a timer set for three minutes. I would sit on a battered couch while the kettle boiled, focusing on my breath's cool entrance at the nostrils, warm exit. Three minutes felt eternal at first. My leg twitched, nose itched, inbox beckoned. Gradually, something tilted. The itch still came, but I didn't need to scratch it instantly. The breath became an anchor. Thoughts drifted, yet I learned I could watch them sail by without boarding every ship.

It's crucial to mention that stillness does not guarantee bliss. Some sessions stirred old grief, unresolved arguments, childhood embarrassments. [Sudarshan Kriya by Pt Ravi Shankar, Art of Living] But encountering those ghosts in a space of nonreaction allowed them to air out. The storm inside began to organise itself like clouds after rain, revealing blue sky. I was stunned by how much room remained once the mental furniture was rearranged.

Remembering the Whisper

I sometimes picture humanity as a grand orchestra, warming up. Instruments tuning, cacophony rising, each player eager, anxious, competitive. Suddenly, a conductor steps onto the podium and lifts the baton. For a brief inhale, absolute silence reigns. In that hush, everyone realises they are part of the same composition. The music then begins, not chaotic but cohesive. *Stillness is the baton lift. It does not negate the music–it prepares the possibility for harmony.*

Ancient traditions passed down techniques for tuning. The mantra *Om* in Hinduism is a lighthouse for wandering minds. They knew the brain loves repetition, so they embedded meaning within rhythm. Neuroscientists now confirm that rhythmic chanting evens out heartbeats and stimulates the vagus nerve, ushering the body into rest-and-digest mode.

Yet beneath technique lies a subtler teaching we are not the storm of triggers. We are the sky that holds them.

Mystics have called that sky soul, spirit, consciousness, *Atman*, and within.

Labels vary, experience endures. When we glimpse the sky even once–maybe during a commute, maybe while washing dishes, maybe atop a mountain–we carry a scent of home. The world will still whip itself into whirlwinds, but part of us has learned where the quiet is stored.

Conclusion: Hearing It Again

So why are we restless? Because the machinery of the mind evolved for vigilance and survived by predicting danger. Because culture decorates that vigilance with flashy baubles, monetising every flicker of attention. Because we inherit ancient habits that try to solve inner tension with outer activity. Yet the deeper answer is startlingly simple- we've forgotten to listen for the ancient whisper beneath the noise.

The good news is that forgetting implies the possibility of remembering.

There's a poem by one of my favourite people, Rajesh Tailang Sir, actor and poet, which is apt in this context:

> "...याद रहता है कि मैं तुम्हें भूल चुका हूँ,
> बस मेरी कुर्सियों के हत्थे याद करते हैं तुम्हारी कोहनियों को।
> मेरी बालकनी की रेलिंग याद करती हैं तुम्हारी एड़ियों को,
> दरवाज़े के कुंडे याद करते हैं तुम्हारी हथेलियों को,
> चाय का कप याद करता है तुम्हारी उँगलियों की गरमाहट को,
> मुझे हर वक़्त याद रहता है कि मैं भूल चुका हूँ तुमको।"

In the chapters ahead, we will explore how busyness becomes a badge of honour, how our devices train compulsive loops, how faith outshines fear, and how ordinary acts shimmer with sacredness. But every insight rests on the foundation we laid today– the recognition of the restless mind and the knowledge that it can be met with a patient, spacious presence.

Carry that silence with you to the next chapter, where we'll confront the cult of doing and ask why we equate motion with meaning.

For now, let's savour one last breath, in and out, and notice the ancient whisper growing just a little clearer.

Chapter 2

The Cult of Doing: How We Worship Busyness

A Bridge from the Ancient Whisper

When we closed the last page, we may have heard that faint, ancient whisper still echoing in our ears– the reminder that our minds have always been restless, that even rishis beneath banyan trees had to coax their thoughts into silence. Yet knowing why we are restless is only half the revelation. The other half confronts us the moment we wake up, swipe the alarm off our phones, and notice a familiar pulsation of urgency– I need to get moving.

We live in an age that does not merely tolerate activity– it idolises it. Busyness has become both armour and ornament. We adorn ourselves with packed calendars the way a medieval knight once strapped on chainmail, hoping it will shield him from the arrows of inadequacy. In this chapter we will lay that armour on the ground, examine its dents and scratches, and ask with equal parts curiosity and courage whether we might walk more freely without it.

The New Idol on the Table

A few months ago, I caught an early-morning flight from Bengaluru to Delhi. I was seated beside the XYZ Company's product manager who worked for a shining, wildly funded start-up. His phone never left his palm, from take-off to landing. Between bites of the airline's idli, he was triaging Slack messages, approving design mock-ups, and confirming back-to-back meetings he would sprint to the moment the plane's wheels kissed the tarmac. When the captain announced the descent, he exhaled with the zeal of a marathon runner spotting the finish line.

"I'm slammed till midnight," he said, almost proudly. "Seventy-hour weeks, but that's the game." Then he added the modern mantra, "If I'm not hustling, someone else will."

I asked him what he would do if the start-up suddenly vanished– servers wiped, investors gone just like that... itni der mein we had become friends na... toh pooch liya. He blinked, confused, as though I had asked what he would do if gravity stopped working. His identity had fused itself to ceaseless motion– stillness felt not merely unfamiliar but existentially threatening.

This conversation plays out everywhere in co-working spaces lit by digital slogans, on social media where rise-and-grind posts collect likes like confetti, even in spiritual communities that quietly measure worth by how many retreats, workshops, and "offerings" one can cram into a weekend.

Activity pretends as essence. Doing confuses being.

From Tapasya to Treadmills

Ancient Hindu wisdom never condemned action. In fact, the Bhagavad Gītā elevates *karma yoga*, the path of selfless action, as a legitimate road to liberation. But it makes a crucial distinction modern culture tends to skip–action must emerge from inner alignment, not from intoxicating restlessness.

When Prince Arjuna trembles on the battlefield of Kurukshetra, overwhelmed by doubt, Lord Krishna does not tell him to flee into meditation caves. Krishna encourages action, yet anchors it in a paradox- "You have a right to perform your prescribed duties, but you are not entitled to the fruits of your actions." That single verse (Gītā 2.47) slices through the cult of busyness like a sharp wind. The Gītā acknowledges the necessity of engaging with the world, but it severs our identity from outcomes. If results are no longer an obsession, the quality of busyness dissipates.

One can act with vigour yet remain inwardly unhurried–*Nishkama Karma*, action without clinging.

Contrast this with the modern treadmill. Outcomes are everything–metrics, click-through rates, performance reviews, follower counts. Because outcomes define self-worth, activity becomes compulsory.

We sprint not toward truth but toward relief from insecurity. The treadmill accelerates, and we call it progress.

My Own Collision with Hustle

There was a year of my life, ironically, just after the meditation, The Art of Living retreat, when I hurtled into the 'productivity mania'. I maintained two jobs, acting in serials on weekdays and writing as a ghostwriter for others and still found time to post inspirational quotes about "being present." My body, wiser than my ego, finally staged a mutiny. One humid afternoon I fainted while buying vegetables. The doctor's prescription was humiliatingly simple:

"Sleep eight hours, walk slowly, and chew your food."

I remember sitting on the bed that night, IV drip still fresh in my arm, and rereading a verse from the Īśā Upanisad:

ईशा वास्यमिदं सर्वं
यत्किञ्च जगत्यां जगत् ।
तेन त्यक्तेन भुञ्जीथा
मा गृधः कस्य स्विद्धनम् ॥

"All this–whatever moves in this moving world–belongs to the Lord. Therefore, enjoy through renunciation. Do not covet anyone's wealth."

The text is barely eighteen verses long, yet it felt like thunder rolling through my skull. I realised I had wanted time itself, hoarded it, and spent it in the same frantic gesture. Not for love, not for service, but for the high that comes from feeling indispensable.Healing required a total reorientation.

I began to treat gaps in my schedule as sacred spaces rather than liabilities. I said no to extra projects and yes to unhurried tea with my mother. The productivity gurus would claim I lost momentum. But in the silence that rushed in, I heard my own heartbeat again, and it sounded suspiciously like freedom.

Anatomy of Modern Busyness

What exactly feeds this relentless pace?

First, there is technological acceleration. A farmer could gift his son a plough, but today we gift our children smartphones that can attract every kind of distraction.

Second, we inherited a marketplace morality–value equals output.

Third, spiritual amnesia–forgetting that life already is sacred– drives us to paint meaning on the outside of experience, like paintings on a temple wall.

Sanskrit offers three distinct qualities of energy, the gunas: *sattva* (purity), *rajas* (activity), and *tamas* (inertia). When rajas dominates, motion becomes its own drug. The mind flickers like a candle in the wind. Judgment blurs, cravings intensify, sleep shortens. Sound familiar? Rajas characterizes not merely individuals but entire civilizations.

Walk through a global airport at 5 am and we can feel the rajas crackling in fluorescent lights and anxious footsteps. Yet Hindu texts never demonise rajas. They view it as necessary at certain stages–the seed pushes through soil only by *rajasic* force. What the sages caution against is identification. When rajas becomes who we are, we lose the freedom to shift into sattvic stillness or *tamasic* rest. We become mono-flavoured beings, addicted to speed.

The Myth of Multi-Tasking and the Vrttis (Circles) of the Mind

Neuroscience now echoes what Patañjali's 'Yoga Sūtra' asserted millennia ago–the mind does not truly multi-task, it oscillates rapidly between objects, producing the illusion of simultaneity.

Patañjali describes mental fluctuations as vrttis, which disturb inner clarity.

Neuroscientists describe attentional residue. Different tongues, same truth.

I once watched a friend prepare for an important presentation while texting three group chats, monitoring crypto prices, and listening to a podcast at 1.5× speed. After twenty minutes, he looked up, glassy-eyed, and confessed he couldn't remember a single sentence of the document.

The yogic antidote is "Ekāgratā"–single-pointed focus–revered as both a cognitive skill and a spiritual posture.

The moment we stop slicing consciousness into shards, a quiet potency appears. Time feels generous again.

Sacred Slowness in the Scriptures

Hindu texts and scriptures like Vishnupuranas and Shivpuranas, etc. supply images of deliberate, unhurried power. Think of the tortoise *Kūrma* supporting Mount *Mandara* during the *Samudra Manthan* (churning of the cosmic ocean). Vishnu takes the form of an ancient reptile, hardly the poster child of hustle, yet without his patient stillness the nectar of immortality could never be surfaced.

Or look at the river Ganga descending from the heavens. The gods trembled at her force, afraid she would shatter Earth. Only Lord Shiva, seated in deep meditation, could bear her flood in his tangled locks, allowing her waters to trickle down, gently.

The narrative is not subtle but clear–speed without containment destroys while motion tempered with stillness nourishes.

Such narratives invite us to shift from chronological time (*kāla*) to sacred time (*ritam*). In sacred time, one moment of wholehearted attention outweighs hours of scrambled activity.

The Upaniṣhads declare, 'that which is infinite is enjoyable– without infinite, there is no bliss.'

Infinity is not a quantity but depth of presence inhabiting a single breath.

A Corporate Cautionary Tale

Let's step from sacred texts into a boardroom in Mumbai. A friend of mine, Vibha, rose swiftly to become vice president at a multinational bank. Her calendar was carved into fifteen-minute blocks, a mosaic of urgency. She began skipping lunch, then yoga class, then family dinners. Promotions arrived but so did migraines. During the Diwali vacations, her doctor found early signs of hypertension. Advised by her doctor, she took a sabbatical, more from medical necessity than spiritual yearning.

While visiting her ancestral village, she spent mornings on the veranda with her family, watching the sun lift over fields. One dawn her father recited a verse from the Bhaja Govindam, Adi Shankaracharya's lyrical plea to awaken from worldly trance–

"Time plays and life ebbs away, yet the storm of desire never ends."

Vibha felt the line pierce her ribcage soon after. She decided to redesign her life around *kṣhama* (patience) and *saucha* (inner purity). When she returned to Mumbai, she negotiated a four-day workweek, hired and mentored two juniors, and reclaimed evenings for kalarippayattu classes. Her output decreased, but her creativity soared. Within months the bank began to replicate her workflow across teams, realising that sustainable pace could still yield profit.

Rajas balanced by sattva becomes wisdom in action.

The Inner Metrics That Matter

If modern culture measures life by how many plates we keep spinning, scripture invites a subtler metric–*antar-sukha* (inner contentment).

Krishna describes the sage as one who finds joy "within himself, by himself." That said, it does not negate outer roles– it simply relocates the source of worth.

Let's try this as an experiment. At the end of a 14-hour day, instead of asking yourself "Did I finish everything?", re-arrange the question: "Was I present in anything, any moment?" Even a single mindful conversation can outweigh a cascade of frantic emails. Presence composts hours into depth.

Re-imagining Productivity

There is, admittedly, legitimate satisfaction in craft, in work that serves others. The key is orientation.

In Karma Yoga the hand moves, the heart offers, the ego steps aside. Activity transforms into worship.

The *Nāradīya Bhakti Sūtra* goes further– "Whatever we do, do it as an offering to the Lord." When the boundary between office and table dissolves, the dichotomy of busy vs. spiritual collapses. Suddenly, sending a well-crafted spreadsheet can carry the same fragrance as lighting a lamp. Yet offering requires margin.

A pot filled to the brim spills when carried. Similarly, a tightly packed schedule leaves no room for adhyātma (self-remembering).

This is to embrace what I call "holy inefficiency." That means intentionally allowing spacious pauses, knowing that in those gaps the subconscious arranges insights, much like Shiva's quiet absorption rearranges cosmic energies.

Rituals of Pause

The Vedas open with the mystical syllable AUM–a sound that contains both vibration and silence. Without the silence surrounding it, the mantra would be noise.

On my own time, I carve miniature silences. Before a Zoom call I close my eyes, inhale slowly, and whisper Śāntiḥ, Śāntiḥ, Śāntiḥ–"peace, peace, peace." The meeting often unfolds with surprising ease, as though everyone subconsciously sensed the micro-ritual.

A sculptor in my town, Bhilai, Chhattisgarh, once told me that he never begins chiselling a granite idol without first washing his hands and gazing at the blank stone until his heartbeat slows. When I asked why, he smiled, "If I'm in a hurry, the chisel slips."

Our lives are no different. Hurry is a dull blade.

The Courage to Say No

Behind chronic busyness lurks the fear of disappointing others or, worse, losing relevance. Saying no can feel like social suicide. The Mahābhārata, however, praises firm discernment–vivek. When Yudhiṣṭhira gambles away kingdom and kin, the fault is not in playing dice but in forgetting discernment. He says yes when a firm disagreement could have preserved dharma (duty).

Each invitation we decline is an act of creative destruction–clearing psychic clutter so that our actual dharma can bloom. Declining certain pathways honours the ones destiny already etched inside us.

A sannyāsin renounces the worldly sphere–a householder renounces excess. Both are forms of tapas (heat) that purifies.

I keep a handwritten note above my table from the day I did finish The Art of Living course:

"May my choices mirror my worship."

It reminds me that if I worship busyness, I become the noise. If I worship presence, I become a tuning fork for stillness.

Communal Busyness and Collective Liberation

The cult of doing is rarely a solo enterprise– it is a collective chant. A single employee who adopts a saner rhythm may face suspicion– "Are they not ambitious?" In the Rāmāyaṇa, when the monkey army wonders how to leap the ocean to Lanka, *Jāmbavān* gently reminds Hanuman of his dormant power.

Sometimes we need friends who recall our true capacity for both silence and stride.

Lately, I planned on hosting monthly "Unhustle Circles," gatherings where all my professional friends– like actors, writers, and directors– share one practice that helped them slow down. Stories breed permission. Busyness loosens its grip not merely through individual epiphanies but through cultural reinforcement.

Vivekananda said, "Seek solitude once a year. In silence we will know what to keep and what to discard."

All the fun, with relaxation as a bonus!

Death as the Final Deadline

No discussion of hurry is complete without remembering the ultimate cut-off point.

Kathopaniṣad personifies Death as *Yama*, the cosmic instructor who tells *Nachiketa*, "The way to the good and the way to the pleasant lead in different directions." Busyness usually chases the pleasant-wisdom selects the good, often at a slower gait.

Sometimes I feel tempted to overload my week and then I visualize my own funeral pyre on the ghats of Varanasi. The image is not morbid–it is liberating.

Mortality clarifies priorities. It pushes us from the cult of doing toward the art of meaningful doing.

A Practice in the Margins

Tonight, before sleep claims you, try lighting a small candle or simply place your phone on airplane mode. Sit beside whatever flicker remains, flame or breath, and ask, 'Who am I without tasks?' Do not seek an answer–here, the asking is the meditation. In the hush that follows, feel the way time softens, like butter melting under the sun. That softness is our original pace.

The *Taittirīya Upaniṣad* describes *ānanda*, supreme bliss, not as an extravagant achievement but as layers of satisfaction beneath the roles we perform.

Peel away the role of an employee, peel away the role of a parent, even peel away the role of a seeker, and there remains a luminous emptiness that is simultaneously full. Reaching that centre does not require quitting our job. It requires non-participation from the frenzy that insists our job defines us.

From Cult to Culture

It is fashionable to attend productivity workshops but rarer is the courage to host a "slowness summit" in our own living room.

Try this–invite children for a slow breathing session of three minutes. Watch the dog wag its tail without you scrolling. Let rice boil without multitasking.

You will find that "Culture is stitched in these unnoticed moments".

When the sage Vyasa composed the eighteen voluminous Puranas, he still felt restless. His guru Narada advised him to sing the glories of devotion. Only then did Vyasa find peace. Production alone could not satisfy. It was the intention that lifted production into prayer.

We, too, can type code, bake bread, and negotiate contracts–yet if the undercurrent is hurried striving, the soul stays parched. Inject devotion, and the same acts quench thirst.

A Soft Transition toward the Tyranny of Thoughts

Slowly, we have walked the perimeter of busyness and peered into its engine room.

We have seen that the cult of doing is less about external tasks and more about internal compulsion.

In the next chapter we will dive even deeper, past schedules and into the labyrinth of the mind itself, where thoughts swirl like a cyclone, dictating pace before a single step is taken.

For now, just close this chapter the way a priest might close the temple gate at dusk–gently, with a whisper of gratitude. Feel the click of the latch. The world outside remains busy, but inside the courtyard of our awareness a lamp is lit, steady and calm, waiting to illuminate whatever arises next.

Chapter 3

Noise in Head: The Tyranny of Thoughts

When the Inner Radio Never Shuts Off

We wake up before the alarm. The room is quiet, but inside our skull a conversation has already started. Did I reply to that e-mail? Why did my director look at me that way during the meeting? I really need to exercise today. Oh, the rent is due. One anxious thread braids itself around another until a single moment has turned into a thousand moments, none of which we are actually living in.

In the previous chapter we examined how society glamourizes busyness, turning our calendars into crowded temples where we worship productivity. But even if we clear an afternoon, silence our notifications, and sit by the window, the deeper hustle continues. It happens inside.

This chapter is about that storm, the tyranny of thoughts, and how ancient scripture, contemporary neuroscience, and a handful of everyday experiments can help us cross the swirling waters to the far shore of quiet.

Arjuna's Confession: A Window from the GEETA

Arjun, in the sixth chapter of the Bhagavad Geeta asks:

"O Krishna! The mind is restless, turbulent, powerful, and obstinate. I think it is as difficult to control as the wind."

Notice what the legendary warrior does not say. He does not complain about the enemy's chariots, or the weight of his bow. The real adversary sits between his very ears.

Even at the brink of mythology's most fateful battle, Arjuna's primary experience is psychological turmoil, the interior quarrel of ethical doubt and unceasing inference.

Krishna's reply here is gentle and precise. Yes, he agrees, the mind is fickle. Yet, he adds, "abhyasa" and "vairagya" (practice and dispassion) can steady it.

The Geeta does not deny the power of thoughts–it offers tools to make the best of these very thoughts.

That single teaching will rebound across centuries, resurfacing in Patanjali's Yoga Sutras and in every cognitive-behavioural therapist's office where a patient is taught to name rather than obey the stories spinning in the head.

Some readers approach scriptures expecting cosmic fireworks–gods descending on clouds, miracles of epic scale. The real miracle is subtler–a mind capable of recognizing its own agitation and choosing not to amplify it. Whenever I see Arjuna's sentence printed on a page, I hear a contemporary voice beneath it–a software engineer who can't detach from project Slack channels on weekends, a mother repeating a single awkward conversation, a student doom-scrolling through bad news. The battlefield is now a bedroom, a boardroom, an anxious commute.

Yet the counsel is identical–practice and dispassion.

A Brief Tour of the Modern Brain

Let's step briefly into an MRI lab. A volunteer lies inside the machine. She is given no task but to rest. Almost immediately, certain brain areas ignite–the medial prefrontal cortex, posterior cingulate cortex, inferior parietal lobule.

Researchers label this pattern "task-negative," because it appears when external tasks are absent.

But subjectively something is very active–mental time travel, speculation, evaluation–a ceaseless monologue that cognitive scientists describe as self-referential processing.

Left unconstrained, this default mode can be a creative ally.

Daydreaming seeds innovation–autobiographical memory knits identity. Yet the same network, studies show, becomes hyperactive in depression, rumination, and anxiety disorders.

The mind is both the sculptor and vandal of its own architecture.

When I read these journals, I imagine a council of ancient sages nodding. Thousands of years ago they lacked MRI images, yet their phenomenological lens was razor sharp.

The Yoga Sutras define yoga as "chitta vritti nirodha"–the calming of the fluctuations of consciousness. Remove the Sanskrit and insert modern slangcalm the mental browser tabs. Same insight, different code.

My Own Hour of Frenzy

Allow me a confession. A few years ago, while drafting this book on mindfulness, I booked a retreat in hills with serene beauty and calm surroundings where I expected birdsong and clarity, perhaps a spiritual halo. Instead I found spotty Wi-Fi, a leaking roof, and my own unfiltered head. With no phone service, no partner and no deadlines, I assumed peace would arrive like an Amazon package–scheduled and predictable. Instead, I discovered a carnival. Old regrets replayed like unpopular songs on shuffle. Imaginary arguments with people I adored. Fantasies of future interviews in which I sounded intelligent and wise.

The ability of the mind to replicate stress with no external stimulus shocked me. I kept looking at my wristwatch, but the hands moved through molasses. By the night, I realised that what terrified me was not the absence of input, but exposure. I was alone with the noise-maker behind the curtain.

The second morning, out of exhaustion, I sat on the deck and said aloud–"Okay, do your worst." For the next hour, thoughts surged–memories of middle-school humiliation, worries about money, and fear that people I love might die before I apologized for some minor slight. Each thought appeared like a wave and collapsed. After forty minutes perhaps, the waves grew translucent. I noticed the sky rather than the commentary about the sky. Wind meshed with breath. A red-tailed hawk drifted overhead and I watched it instead of composing a metaphor about watching it.

I do not claim enlightenment.

The carnival returned half an hour later, though the volume had dipped significantly. But I learned an intuitive lesson–

"Stillness is not a deletion of thought–it's widening of awareness until thoughts occupy the same space as clouds–visible, dynamic, and incapable of harming the sky itself."

The Startup Founder Who Lost His Mind–and Found It

Jishan, a thirty-three-year-old founder of a startup, personified speed. He wore a smart watch that vibrated each time a user completed a transaction on his app. During a single coffee meeting, his wrist buzzed so often the table felt like it was experiencing tremors. "Good problem to have," he joked, yet the smile twitched nervously.

Six months later, Jishan collapsed in the office restroom, not from cardiac arrest but from panic.

Paramedics found him curled on the marble floor, convinced he was dying. Medical tests showed normal vital signs.

The diagnosis–acute anxiety disorder.

Jishan's investors recommended therapy. His mother recommended the *Shiva Mahima Stotram*.

Jishan chose a ten-day silent Vipassana retreat, partly because no cell phones were allowed–a condition he suspected would please both the therapists and the mother.

The first two days were tormenting. "My legs hurt, sure," he told me later, "but the worst pain was the brain." He described how thoughts refused the silence. Marketing projections, his ex-girlfriend's laughter, the scent of espresso, the uncertainty of funding–everything erupted during each hour of seated meditation.

On the fourth evening, Jishan experienced a shift. While focusing on his breath, he noticed that his thoughts of freezing hirings appeared, swelled, and faded. In the faint gap that followed, he said, he felt "empty but alive."

The next thought arrived but now he could track the arc like watching a runner on a track rather than being dragged behind the runner.

By the tenth day, Jishan reported seeing thoughts the way astronomers see meteors–streaks across a wider backdrop. The stars were still there–the constancy of awareness.

When he returned to Bengaluru, he redesigned his notification algorithm so his watch buzzed only once an hour with a batch summary. He also instituted a company policy–every employee receives a quarterly silent day. Investors were sceptical until retention rates improved.

"Silence was good business," Jishan laughed. "But more importantly, silence was good."

The Myth of Controlling Thoughts

A common misconception–reinforced by social media images of lotus-shaped serenity–is that spiritual practice eradicates thinking. Hindu scripture never promises a mental desert. Krishna does not instruct Arjuna to annihilate the wind–He advises learning to sail with it. The Bhagavata Purana describes sages who witness the universe emerging and dissolving inside consciousness–as a constant change against the canvas of changelessness.

They are not blank–they are spacious.

Similarly, neuroscience experiments show that trying to suppress a thought intensifies its recurrence. One should not imagine a pink elephant and then be surprised when the elephant gallops through every synaptic corridor.

The goal, then, is not the strangulation of cognition but the right relationship.

I like the image Swami Vivekananda used while commenting on Patanjali. He compared the mind to a drunken monkey who has been stung by a scorpion. Add theological passion and the monkey becomes possessed by a demon. We cannot sober the animal by shouting. But we can surely build a treehouse so that while the monkey chatters down, we watch without fear.

Breath: The Oldest Remote Control

Pause now.

Feel the air folding into our lungs. Notice texture–the slight coolness spraying against nasal walls and the warmth as it spirals outward across our upper lip. Nothing mystical about it but the simple chemistry of oxygen and carbon dioxide. And yet, inhalation is one of the few bodily functions that obeys both voluntary and involuntary systems. That duality makes breath the perfect bridge.

In the Shiva Purāṇa, a verse describes prāṇa (life force) as the bow by which the seeker launches awareness toward the bull's-eye of the Self. Studies have found that deliberate, slow breathing reduces activity in the locus coeruleus, a brain nucleus that triggers the stress response.

The conclusion matches what yogis have long known: exhale longer than you inhale, and the nervous system settles happily into parasympathetic gear.

Try it–four counts in, six counts out, repeated a dozen times. Thoughts, noticing the absence of fuel, often soften their artillery. I have used this method while waiting to give public talks. Minutes before walking on stage, adrenaline roars. I breathe in for the count of four, out for eight. The body receives a memo–situation under control. The crowd does not shrink, but my thoughts lose their commander.

Mantra: Sound Fence for a Wandering Mind

It is said that, "Where breath engages physiology, mantra employs vibration."

The Rig Veda proclaims, "In the beginning was Vac-the Word."

Early sages uncovered that certain phonetics resonate with neural patterns, shepherding attention. The most famous, of course, is Aum, three syllables woven into one cosmic hum.

During my cabin retreat, after a half-pleasant hour of sky-watching thoughts, I made my chai and found myself humming 'Om' under my breath. The hum anchored me to the kettle's hiss. Each time a new worry threatened to hijack perception, I slipped the mantra onto the tongue. It functioned like a shepherd's crook, tugging stray sheep's attention back to centre.

Science again provides a parallel narrative. Functional imaging of novice meditators chanting shows deactivation in the amygdala, the brain's alarm bell. Meanwhile, the hippocampus, gatekeeper of memory, lights up. In simpler terms, mantra reduces emotional turbulence and improves situational mapping.

The Puranas would describe this as sattva increasing, the mind becoming luminous and buoyant.

Naming the Weather: A Tiny Practice

Right now, pause reading and glance inward. Without changing anything, identify the dominant tone of our mental landscape.

Is it anxious planning? Mild irritation? Random nostalgia? Give it a one-word weather report–foggy, gusty, stagnant.

Labeling affects ownership.

When we say, "Ah, anxiety," we create an object-subject distinction. The sensation is real but not identical to the one who observes it. This simple shift, popularized in mindfulness courses, echoes a verse from the *Katha Upaniṣad*– "The Self is the rider, intellect the charioteer, mind the reins."

Recognize the reins as reins, and suddenly we are the rider, not the clattering wheels.

During therapy sessions, suddenly a thought arrived in my mind– what if my partner leaves me?– and immediately the playlist "tu menu chadd chaleya...." was playing. I didn't stop the song. I was like, the mind, like Spotify, will auto-select next tracks, but awareness keeps the volume manageable.

My Father's Evening Walk

Growing up, I saw my father pacing the rooftop every night after dinner. No smartwatch counted his steps.

He called it "digesting the day." Hands clasped behind his back, he stared at the stars... Bhilai waale ghar ki chhat.

One evening I joined him, aged fourteen, agitated by exam results. He listened and said, "Thoughts are passengers, we are the station."

Then he pointed at the railway tracks beyond our house, shimmering with heat.

"The trains arrive," he said, "but the platform does not chase them."

At fourteen, I rolled my eyes. Now I realize he was borrowing from the *Maitri Upanishad*-

"Mind is the unsteady chariot– see it, and we can stand on the ground."

Papa never quoted scripture- he embodied it in a slow, repetitive walk. I found a worn out copy of the Bhagwat Geeta on his bedside table, each margin scribbled with notes.

The final page bore one sentence– "What returns to silence was never separate from it."

The Neuroscience of Letting Go

Recent studies showed that experienced meditators display reduced activity in the posterior cingulate cortex during practice, corresponding with a subjective feeling of "effortless awareness."

When researchers interrupted them and asked what was happening, they often replied, "Nothing in particular, just resting in an open presence.

"The key term is effortless. Effort to offload thought can become paradoxically another thought loop.

Here we can appreciate Krishna's second tool– vairagya, dispassion. It is not indifference but ungluing.

We do not push thoughts away– we allow them to float until they pop like soap bubbles. The moment a bubble catches our eye, admire the rainbow sheen, then let the air do its natural work.

How Social Media Supercharges the Tyrant

Let us take a brief detour to the digital realm, because our gadgets intensify mental chatter. Each swipe offers a new stimulus, new storyline, new invitation to think, evaluate, compare. The dopamine loop is not merely chemical– it trains the default mode network to crave novelty.

After an hour on Instagram, the contemplative mind resembles a toddler fed cake– wired, cranky, unable to nap.

Ancient texts warned of this without foreseeing screens.

The *Bhāgavata Purāṇa* lists six enemies of the soul– *kāma, krodha, lobha, moha, mada, mātsarya*– desire, anger, greed, delusion, pride, envy.

Every scroll can trigger all six within fifty seconds.

Recognition is the first buffer.

When we notice envy prick our gut, label it– "mātsarya-storm alert."

Then breathe. The emotion may not vanish, but we can regain captaincy.

Crafting a Daily Window of Stillness

The most common objection I hear is time scarcity.

People request a hack– the ninety-second meditation, the three-breath miracle.

Those are useful spark plugs, but the engine still needs oil. The Upanishads describe sādhanā as a river eroding rock through persistent flow. Begin with ten minutes. Same chair, same corner, same hour. Repetition matters because it trains the brain's predictive coding. When we sit, neurons fire in recognition–oh, the stillness routine.

Choose an anchor–breath, mantra, visual candle flame. Do not curse the circus of thought that follows. Infants cry–we rock them, we do not scold their existence. Each time we realise we were lost in a story, celebrate. Awareness just flexed its muscle.

I have followed this for a long time. Some mornings the practice feels like sweeping dust in a windstorm. Other mornings a crystal interval arrives when the world exhales. Both outcomes are fine.

What matters is showing up, because practice carves neural grooves that widen during crises.

When my mother was hospitalised last year, after being diagnosed with uterine cancer, my mind wanted to sprint into catastrophic films. The practice intervened, not with pep talk, but with space. I could hold her hand

and be there, not trapped in futures that might never arrive.

If an alien species observed humanity, it might assume our brains were radios stuck between stations– static, half-songs, bursts of advertisement. Yet the same brain is capable of chamber music. Remember a time– perhaps walking by the beach at dusk– when everything fell into place, not because external conditions were perfect, but because internal commentary receded to a whisper. That capacity is not rare– it is default.

Noise is not the substrate but an overlay.

Rama, disenchanted with royal life, complains of world-weariness. Sage Vasistha replies by leading him through stories that reveal the mind's power to paint heaven and hell. At the end Rama sees the world anew, not devoid of thought but transparent to being.

There is no grand miracle, only a softening.

In the next chapter, we will explore the art of moving through life at a pace that honours awareness rather than stifles it. Slowness is not the opposite of productivity- it is the soil from which meaningful action sprouts.

For now, remember Arjuna's confession and Krishna's cure– practice and gentle detachment.

Tomorrow morning, when the inner radio begins its broadcast, sit for a moment before touching the volume knob.

Listen without obeying. The wind is strong, yes, but there is enough sky to hold it.

Chapter 4

The Art of Sacred Slowness

A Breath Between Thoughts

When we closed the last chapter, we were standing in the thick jungle of our own minds, watching thoughts swing from branch to branch, like a troupe of caffeine-fuelled monkeys. We might have noticed something surprising in that exercise and the very moment we observed those thoughts, a thin ribbon of quiet appeared among them. That quiet may have lasted for half a second– more or less. But whatever its length, it was spacious enough for peace to perch upon it. This chapter is about widening that ribbon and stretching it until calm is no longer an accidental visitor but a permanent resident in our inner landscape.

I call that widening "sacred slowness." It is not the cultural slowness of hitting the snooze button or binge-watching an entire series over a weekend while pizza boxes accumulate like geological strata.

Sacred slowness is intentional, awake, reverent.

It is the deliberate choice to move, speak, eat, and think at a tempo that allows our soul to keep up with our body. Picture a violinist who stops racing through a complicated piece and instead lingers on every note until the wood of the instrument seems to inhale and exhale with her.

Slowness turns living into music. It also terrifies the modern ego.

We tie our worth to speed: the number of e-mails answered before breakfast, the steps counted by a fitness band, the side hustles proudly announced on LinkedIn. The invitation to slow down can therefore feel like a demotion. What if we discover that life carries on quite well without our frantic micro-management? Worse, what if we discover that underneath the noise, uncomfortable feelings lie waiting: grief, boredom, and longing.

These fears are natural. Yet beneath them, another intuition glimmers- there must be another rhythm available, one in which life still moves, but it moves like a river rather than a firehose.

In the next pages, I want to you to explore that rhythm with me

Ready? Slip off your shoes. Feel the floor under your feet. Let's walk, and not run.

Why Slowing Down Heals the Brain

Before we go further, let's invite science to the table, because the sceptical part of us might whisper, "Sure. Monks, sages, and rishis can slow down– they have no bills to take care of." Fair point. Yet slowness is not a luxury item. It is a biological imperative.

Our nervous systems evolved in a world where changes unfolded over seasons, not days. A few centuries ago, the fastest message could travel only as swiftly as a horse could gallop. Today, we can watch the stock market rise and fall in micro-seconds. Each ping on our phone tells the amygdala, our brain's threat detector, that something requires immediate action. This relentless stimulation locks the body into sympathetic overdrive– heart accelerates, cortisol floods, muscles tense.

Over time, chronic stress dulls the prefrontal cortex, the region responsible for empathy, creativity, and moral reasoning. We become clever animals but lose our wisdom.

Slowness, conversely, recruits the parasympathetic nervous system, often called "rest and digest."

When our breathing deepens and our movements unhurriedly match it, the vagus nerve sends a signal up to the brainstem- "All clear. Lower the drawbridge." The heart rate eases. The mind shifts from scanning for danger to scanning for beauty. Neurotransmitters such as serotonin and GABA step forward, soothing anxiety. In these slower brain waves-alpha and theta-novel connections spark. That is why people often experience bursts of insight in the shower or on a leisurely walk– the mind, unhurried, finally has bandwidth to rearrange information into patterns.

So when we claim an hour to drink tea in silence, we are not being lazy. We are providing homeostasis to the endocrine orchestra, allowing each instrument to tune itself.

Village Wisdom: The Potter from Durg, Chhattisgarh

To understand sacred slowness in action, let us leave the lab and visit a dusty lane in Durg, Chhattisgarh. One torrid May, I spent an afternoon there, crouched beside a lady potter. Her hands looked older than the rest of her, knotted with veins and flecked with clay that refused to wash off after decades at the wheel. Her process mesmerised me. She did not simply slap clay onto the spinning wheel and shape it like a factory machine.

First, she squatted and pounded the clay with a short wooden bat, humming a devotional song under her breath. Each strike landed with the same cadence. Then she paused, closed her eyes, and pressed her thumb into the mass, assessing its readiness. Only when entirely satisfied did she set it on the wheel. As the wheel spun, she did not race to form the pot. Her fingers roamed over the surface like a lover learning every contour. Occasionally she halted the wheel, tilted her head as though listening to the clay speak, and resumed with microscopic adjustments. In that cramped shed, time elongated.

I asked if the slower method reduced her output. She laughed, a ripple of silver bangles. “Maybe I make fewer pots a day,” she said. “But they almost never crack in the kiln.

Clay remembers the pace of the hands that touched it. If I hurry, it hurries too. Then fire punishes impatience." So does the human heart. Skip the pauses and cracks appear later, often at the worst possible moment– anxiety attacks while driving, tears that ambush us in a public restroom, sharp words that fracture a marriage.

The lady potter's wisdom offers a kind of moral physics– haste bakes brittleness– slowness enforces integrity.

The Slow Walk That Saved a Marriage

Not all lessons in slowness arrive in romantic settings. Sometimes they unfold on suburban sidewalks. A friend of mine, Rajat, was nearly divorced after fifteen years of marriage. He and his wife, Meena, had grown into a life of schedules and mortgages, but had forgotten how to inhabit the same emotional climate. Conversations had devolved into logistics. Intimacy felt like a relic from their honeymoon scrapbook.

A therapist suggested a strange remedy– each evening, take a twenty-minute walk with one rule– walk slower than natural pace. No phone, no power strides, just an amble. They thought it to be absurd but agreed.

The first evening, silence clung to them awkwardly. Cars whisked by while dogs barked from behind the fences. Their feet moved so leisurely they almost tripped on themselves. When Meena reached for Rajat's hand, he flinched, not out of rejection but shock. When was the last time they held hands in public? She laughed softly: something thawed.

In the weeks that followed, those slow walks became a ritual window. Words meandered into spaces previously crammed with urgency. They talked about the books they once loved, the vacations they postponed, and the shadowy fears of middle age. Sometimes they said nothing at all and found the silence companionable. Six months later, they still argued about chores, but the marriage no longer felt like two radio stations broadcasting at incompatible frequencies. Slowness had returned them.

When Rajat told me this story over chai, he shrugged, "turns out the speed of our feet dictated the speed of our hearts,"– almost surprised by his own words. I believe him. We cannot sprint and truly listen at the same time. Listening, like pottery, demands a tempo at which nuance is audible.

Digital World: A Modern Desert

"What about my job?" we might protest. "The world demands speed." Absolutely. Deadlines exist, and some crises require rapid response.

Sacred slowness is not about abolishing speed– it is about restoring choice.

Sages have a dedicated time for meditation and chanting– they are not perpetually lounging under the banana trees. Likewise, we can architect rhythms that include both acceleration and deceleration. The problem is we rarely decelerate on purpose.

Mindful Eating: The Meal That Takes a Lifetime

Perhaps the most intimate terrain for sacred slowness is the act of eating.

Food is how the outside world becomes internal– atoms from sunlit wheat or ocean fish cross the porous boundary of our body and join our cells. Yet, consider how we ate our last lunch.

Did we scroll news feeds between bites? Did we taste the curry? How did the chapati vanish in three wolfish morsels?

At the temples, meals unfolded in silence. The abbot [server]told me, "Chew until rice becomes water." First I mocked the instruction internally-surely rice never dissolves entirely. But curiosity won. One day I counted. It took about fifty chews. Around chew thirty, the texture shifted from grainy to creamy. Around chew forty, a subtle sweetness emerged, a flavour absent when I swallowed ten chomps. I realized I had never truly tasted rice before.

Upon returning home, I introduced a rule-one meal a day, eaten without multitasking at half my usual pace. The results startled me. Portions shrank naturally while satisfaction expanded. Digestion improved. But beyond physiology, a philosophical shift occurred– gratitude. I saw the choreography that led the carrot to my plate- the farmers' dawn labour, the truck driver's long haul, the supermarket clerk's stacking of shelves.

Eating became a communion, not a transaction.

We do not need to chew fifty times- we simply need to be present. Lift the fork as if it carries a universe, because it does.

The Physics of Pause in Creative Work

We may cling to the belief that slowness sabotages productivity. I've found the opposite. While writing this book, I encountered a chapter–ironically, not this one–that refused to flow. I sat for hours forcing sentences that sounded like they belonged to a corporate memo. Frustrated, I shut the laptop and went for a slow walk along the beach. I stopped and leaned on the rock wall, watching a crane stand immobile in the shallows for what felt like ages. Suddenly it speared a fish with surgical precision. That sight burned into me– stillness, then decisive action.

When I returned to my table, the chapter wrote itself.

Neuroscientists would call this the "incubation effect." The conscious mind hits a wall- the subconscious keeps tinkering while we daydream. Yet I prefer the Crane's lesson- move so slowly that the right moment reveals itself, then act. Many artists follow a similar pull.

Slowness is not lack of work–it is the fertile void from which meaningful work arises.

The Objection of Privilege

At this juncture, an important ethical concern surfaces: who can afford to slow down?

A single mother juggling two jobs, a migrant worker paid by output, a student working nights to fund tuition: asking them to slow down may sound like denial of reality. Sacred slowness risks becoming a privilege sermon delivered from cushy armchairs.

Practical Invitations to Slowness

Although I promised no lists, let me weave these suggestions into a story.

Imagine tomorrow as an experiment in tempo. We wake up and, before our feet touch the floor, notice the temperature of the morning air on our face. Rising slowly, we carry that awareness into the shower, feeling the streams drape our shoulders instead of plotting the day. Over breakfast, we choose one sip of 'adrak waali chai' to savour like a wine taster.

Walking to work, we resist overtaking the pedestrian ahead, matching their pace as an act of humility. At lunch, we close the laptop and chew until flavours introduce themselves. In the afternoon meeting, we allow a full second of silence before responding, letting the words settle.

Returning home, we drive in the slow lane, observing the theatrics of the sunset rather than arguing with traffic. Before bed, we place a hand on our chest and ask, "Where did I move too fast today, and can I forgive myself?" Then we sleep without the blue glow of screens, giving dreams the space to compose their nocturnal poetry.

Neuroscience calls this "experience-dependent neuroplasticity": repetitive states become enduring traits. Each moment of deliberate slowness deepens the groove in our brain's vinyl, making it easier for the needle of awareness to follow that track tomorrow.

Slowness is not merely personal wellness– it is a refusal to let the clock of capitalism dictate our moral compass. It is the tempo at which empathy flourishes.

When Slowness Becomes Avoidance

A caution– slowness is sacred only when it serves presence, not escape.

Procrastination can be thought of as mindful pacing. There were afternoons when I lounged on a meditation cushion scrolling mindfulness quotes, telling myself I was honouring slowness while actually I was just dodging work. How do we tell the difference?

Honesty. If, after an hour of "slow research," our body feels heavy and our purpose diluted, we were likely procrastinating.

Authentic slowness leaves us clearer, lighter, and more ready to engage.

Monks, Sages do not sit all day– they also sweep the floor they sit upon, collect alms, and teach novices.

The point of slowness is not eternal inertia, it is, in fact, to charge our action with deliberate wisdom. A river that never moves stagnates. Sacred slowness is closer to a meandering stream– gentle yet progressing and nourishing the banks along the way.

Everything we've discussed funnels into the breath and present from our first cry to our final sigh. Breath can race or walk, and the body obeys its tempo.

Slow breathing– about six cycles per minute– activates baroreceptors that calm the heart.

When anxiety spikes, deliberately elongating the exhale sends a telegram to the brain- condition safe. Nothing external needs to change. Traffic can still honk– inboxes can still overflow. Inside, we stroll even while outside we sit in gridlock.

Once, while waiting to hear biopsy results of my mother, I felt my chest tighten into a Vise. The nurse's footsteps echoed down the hall like incoming doom. I inhaled to a count of four, exhaled to a count of six. It was difficult but after five such breaths, panic softened from a roar to a murmur. The results, when delivered, were benign. But even if they had not been, those breaths granted me composure to receive the news with grace. Our breath is a portable monastery. No travel visa required.

Slowness as Spiritual Time Travel

There is a mystical dimension to slowness that defies measurement. In deep stillness, past and future blur only an endless present remains. Mystics across traditions speak of this timeless now like Buddhists call it the Eternal Now.

I once experienced a fleeting glimpse while sitting by a dock at dusk. Waves lapped wooden posts, gulls wheeled overhead, my breathing matched the tide's rhythm. Suddenly, linear time collapsed. I was a child again, feet dangling in a lake and suddenly, I was an old woman, sighing at my life's dusk. I was all ages at once, anchored in a single heartbeat that felt like eternity. The perception lasted seconds yet altered my entire understanding of mortality.

Slowness cracks open the door to such glimpses. Through that crack, infinity peers back.

Conclusion: Carrying the Lantern Forward

As we set this chapter down, I invite you to feel the wideness of the moment we are inhabiting. Notice how our eyes glide across the words- notice the micro-pauses between sentences. Can we rest inside one of those pauses right now? We have begun, at least in these pages, to step off the moving walkway that hurries the masses toward some mirage of completion. We have met a potter, a sage, a crane, a married couple, perhaps even our own breath, each whispering the same secret–life reveals itself in proportion to the slowness with which we greet it.

The storm of thoughts from earlier chapters still rumbles, but now we carry a lantern of pace.

In the following chapter, we will walk directly into the heart of our era's greatest accelerant– the digital vortex of phones, feeds, and dopamine–and explore how to remain present without retreating to a cave.

Sacred slowness will be our compass. Hold it close.

Chapter 5

Reclaiming Presence in Digital Age

The Slowness We Just Discovered, the Speed We Still Serve

In the previous chapter we tasted slowness like a ripe mango. For a moment the world paused and the juice of attention dripped down our fingers. But as soon as we closed that final page, chances are a notification chimed, the spell broke, and the mind bolted back to its well-worn racetrack. I know the pattern because it is my pattern too.

One evening, having written passionately about mindful walking, I reached for my phone "just to set an alarm for tomorrow's dawn meditation." Fifteen minutes later I was watching a reel of a Himalayan yogi making almond milk.

Slowness evaporated, replaced by the invisible centrifuge of digital velocity.

If stillness is the fragrant agarbatti we lit together in the last chapter, our screens are the open window through which a gust of wind threatens to snuff it out.

This chapter is about closing the window-not to shut the world away, but to steady the flame of presence.

The Glow in the Palm

Close our eyes for a second and picture a commuter train in Mumbai at rush hour. Arms dangle out of the doorway, the car sways, yet almost every passenger clutches a rectangle of light. A labour, still smelling of engine grease, scrolls past cricket highlights; a college student flips through filtered selfies; a grandmother, her sari pinned neatly, listens to the chanting of the Hanuman Chalisa over WhatsApp. Each of them holds an entire universe in the palm.

The Vedas call the thumb (*angushtha*), a symbol of individual soul, and the index finger (*tarjani*), the symbol of the Divine. In the traditional jnana-mudra of meditation, these two fingers touch, completing a circle. Today the same thumb and finger keep swiping instead; the circle broken, the mind scattered outward.

One late monsoon evening, my friend Saanvi, a brilliantly talented sitar player, confided something both ordinary and heartbreaking. She said, "I have not listened to a single alaap fully in months. I start a recording on YouTube, but before the gat begins, another suggestion pops up– 'Check out Ravi Shankar, Woodstock, 1967.' I click. Ten seconds in, a notification from Instagram– 'Someone liked our practice clip.' I check. By the time I return, the alaap has drifted on without me." She added quietly, "I know entire ragas only in fragments now."

Her confession mirrors what many neuroscientists warn: frequent context-switching splinters attention, alters the hippocampus, and reduces what the Gita calls ekagrata– one-pointed focus. The ancients compared a distracted mind to a dog running in circles after its own tail; electrons may have replaced tails, but the spinning feels the same.

Dopamine and the Dance of Distraction

To reclaim presence, we first need to understand how the digital storm hijacks the inner sky. Each ping, badge, and red dot offers a micro-reward. The brain sends a squirt of dopamine, whispering, "Good job. Something new might help us survive."

In the Puranas, rishis speak of indriyas– the senses– as horses. Untrained horses race toward every sudden sound.

Modern neuroscience echoes them– the limbic system is wired to notice novelty, because novelty once signified either predator or prey.

The trouble is that our devices deliver novelty at a rate our nervous system never evolved to handle. A sixteen-year-old receives more novel stimuli before breakfast than a Vedic-forest student encountered in a month. We admire Arjuna's archery, how he could pierce an eye of a rotating wooden fish by focusing only on its reflection in water. Yet we hand that same Arjuna a smartphone and invite him to keep dozens of apps helplessly open. No wonder the bow of attention trembles

Ekagrata: A Word That Holds a Universe

Ekagrata literally means "one-pointedness." Patanjali uses it to define dharana, the sixth limb of yoga, as fixing the mind in one place. But ekagrata is not stern suppression– it is affectionate intimacy with the moment.

Think of a maestro tuning a *tanpura*. She plucks the first string, listens, nudges the wooden peg the width of a fingernail, plucks again. Time disappears. That marriage of ear, fingertip, and vibrating wire is ekagrata.

In the Bhagavad Geeta, Krishna urges Arjuna–tasmat sarveshu kaleshu mam anusmara–therefore, at all times, remember me. Presence is not reserved for Himalayan caves–it is the capacity to recollect the sacred in the middle of Kurukshetra, amidst whirring arrows and shouting warriors. Our battlefield today is the endless feed. The arrows are memes, headlines, ads, fears that we are missing out. The call is the same– remember what we truly are.

The Mahabharata of My Notifications

I used to sneer at digital addiction talks. Then a simple statistic humbled me. My Android phone revealed that, on average, I was unlocking it 112 times a day. That is 112 mini-meditations–except they are directed not toward truth, but toward trifles. One Saturday I decided to log every notification as if it were a Mahabharata character appearing onstage.

"Email from airline: sale on flights"-Adiparva, the opening gambit.

"Breaking news: Celebrity divorce"-Virata Parva, exile in public drama.

"Comment: 'Nice post bro'"-Udyoga Parva, diplomacy through emojis.

"Bank alert: low balance"-Karpara Parva, bones rattling. The comedy soon turned tragic.

By tea-time, I realised most notifications carried neither urgency nor significance. Yet each one pulled a thread from my mental fabric. By evening I felt frayed. That night I revisited a teaching from the Katha Upanishad-

"Like the wide-mouthed highway to ruin is distraction, straight and narrow is the road to liberation."

The verse seemed composed not for gamblers in ancient royal courts but for anyone doom-scrolling past midnight.

The Experiment: Thirty Days Without the Scroll

Saanvi's fragmented ragas stayed with me. We decided on a joint experiment: thirty days off social media. She would delete Instagram and Facebook, I would delete Twitter. We allowed ourselves e-mail for essential work but with notifications disabled.

We called it our "Aranyaka," borrowing the term for the mid-section of the Vedas where householders retreated to the forest to study.

Day one felt comically empty. My thumb, conditioned by years of automatic reach, kept traveling to a blank space where the blue bird icon used to be. I would pick up the phone, stare, sigh, and put it down. Saanvi confessed that the sudden silence unsettled her too. "It's like the tanpura stopped buzzing," she said, "and now every other sound in my house is too loud."

Day three, the restlessness peaked. Without digital snacks, my mind looked for other crumbs: extra chai, random texting, and even nostalgic curiosity about my old photo albums.

Geeta warns of this phase: "when a pleasure is pulled away, the senses revolt, though one may restrain them, the taste lingers."

We almost gave up.

Day seven, something shifted. I felt pockets of boredom open like little verandas. Instead of rushing to fill them, I stepped out and leaned on their railings. A sparrow hopped near an overturned pot, hunting ants. I watched her for five unbroken minutes. The satisfaction was oddly medicinal. Saanvi said she replayed an entire Vilayat Khan alaap, eyes closed, without once touching the sitar strings herself. She listened, only listened. Her teacher later claimed he could hear the difference in her next practice. "Our mind is breathing," he told her.

Day fifteen, I observed a sliver of spaciousness between thoughts. Earlier my attention resembled a crowded market where stall owners shout to outbid each other. Now it felt like stepping onto an early-morning street before the shops open.

The mind still produced wares, but quietly.

Day thirty, I tallied the changes: finished three books I had postponed for months. My dreams became vivid. Conversations lingered, unhurried. When I re-installed Twitter to test my resolve, the timeline appeared garish, impatient. I logged out within minutes, not out of virtue but because my nervous system grimaced.

Saanvi's breakthrough came differently. Mid-month she improvised a new gat in Raga Marwa, spacious and yearning, and posted nothing about it. She simply played for her small living-room audience of two- her mother and the night's first star. She told me later, "I felt as if Marwa was teaching me about dusk rather than me playing Marwa."

Presence had dissolved the boundary between musician and music.

Reclaiming Ritual

When the ancients designed samskaras–rites from birth to death–they understood that human beings drift when untethered. Rituals are intentional buoys strewn across the river of days. Digital rituals can function in the same way, but we must design them consciously or the algorithms will design them for us. I replaced my morning doom-scroll with a tripod of practices rooted in Indian tradition yet translated for city life.

First, I greet dawn in silence, standing by my window facing the faint blush of the east.

In *Rig Veda*, *Usha*, the goddess of dawn, my mother's name ...[I am Blessed] is praised for "opening doors to truth." I simply watch the sky for three breaths, no chanting, no photography. Second, I read aloud a single shloka–any text, sometimes Kabir, sometimes the Geeta–allowing the vibration of Sanskrit or Hindi or English to rinse the mouth. Speaking aloud slows comprehension, like hand-ground spices releasing deeper aroma. Third, I write one sentence in a notebook answering–"What would make today meaningful if this were my last?" The question pierces through vanity projects.

These acts take less time than checking the morning news, but they flavour the entire day. Presence, I discovered, is cumulative–small moments compound like daily drops of sandalwood oil into porous wood, eventually scenting the whole chest.

Sound of Tanpura and the Space Between Notes

Every tradition uses sound to summon presence–church bells, Sufi qawwali, Tibetan bowls.

Indian classical music is unique in how it venerates the drone.

The *tanpura* does not play melody, yet without its gentle Om, the raga cannot blossom. The tanpura teaches that the ground tone, the apparently boring background, is sacred.

Our lives too have a background hum- breathing, heartbeat, gravity.

Screens hijack foreground attention- reclaiming presence begins by apprenticing ourselves to the tanpura of the body.

Try this- Sit quietly, eyes closed, and imagine your spine as the instrument's bridge, our breath as its tune. Each inhalation plucks an invisible string–each exhalation lets it resonate. We are not controlling the breath, only noticing the buzz of life already happening.

Musicians call it 'shuddha swara', pure note. Yogis call it prana. Scientists call it the vagus nerve synchronizing heartbeat and lungs. Different languages, same miracle.

The more we listen, the less the mind begs for loud stimuli.

When I practiced this during our thirty-day fast, I noticed my craving to check messages spiked exactly when I had ignored my inner drone. Digital desire was a distorted echo of legitimate longing for connection–first with myself, then with others. Once I sat acknowledging the inner tanpura for five minutes, the urge abated like a cough suppressed by a sip of warm water.

Practicing Silence in the City

Silence does not require a monastery or any retreat. The Mahabharata's sage Vidura advises King Dhritarashtra to cultivate mauna, the vow of inner quiet, even in court. I live beside a busy flyover in Mumbai– "vo shehar jo kabhi sota nahin." Through my window motorcycles snarl, vendors argue. Yet at dawn, before engines outnumber birds, a hush hovers. I stand barefoot on the balcony's cool tile and let the hush infiltrate my ribcage.

Later in the day I practiced "micro-maun." Finishing a Zoom meeting, I close the laptop and keep my eyes shut for three complete breaths before touching the phone. At traffic lights I roll the window halfway, lower the radio, and watch one inhalation. These slivers feel too small to matter. But remember:

A dam leaks through hairline cracks. Likewise, serenity slips in through narrow chinks of intention.

Saanvi tried her version backstage before a concert at a college festival. Amid amps humming and students giggling, she placed her palms over her ears, gently pressing the tragus, a yogic technique called shanmukhi mudra. It muffled external noise, amplifying the inner omnipresent hiss of blood flow. She emerged calmer, played with fluidity, and later told me, "The audience thought I was meditating for enlightenment. I was just remembering that hearing the world begins by hearing myself."

Detachment, Not Disinterest

A frequent misconception arises: to reclaim presence, we must renounce technology. But the Geeta clarifies that true tyaga–letting go–is internal. Krishna calls the sannyasi one who does his duty without clinging to the fruit, not necessarily one who abandons action. Similarly, we can use devices as tools without letting them use us.

During our experiment, I devised a simple rule. Before opening any app, I ask, "What exactly am I here to do?" If the mind replies with a vague craving–"to pass time"–I delay entry. If the answer is specific–"to message mother train details"–I proceed, finish, and exit. Imagine entering a temple: we remove shoes, light a lamp, bow, and leave. We do not linger gossiping at the sanctum.

Treat mobile apps like sanctums–minus the sanctimony.

Once my work is finished, I sometimes allow playful scrolling, but even then I set a timer for ten minutes, akin to how the sages of the Yoga Vasistha instruct students to let the mind cloud, but observe the clouding. When the bell rings, I close the app and notice bodily sensations–throat dry, eyes sandy. This feedback loop fosters viveka, discernment, sharpening the difference between joy and subtle suffering.

Saanvi reinstalled Instagram after thirty days but uses it only on weekends, often to post a clip of her guru or archival recordings rather than her breakfast. Her student Tara, age nineteen, resisted at first. "Won't followers forget us?" she worried. Saanvi smiled, quoting Kabir:

"Prem gali ati saankari, taame do na samai"– the lane of love is so narrow, two cannot walk side by side.

She explained, "If artistry walks with constant self-promotion, love gets squeezed out." Tara still posts selfies, but now sits for fifteen minutes of alaap practice before every upload. The shift is modest, yet real.

The Evening Lamp: A Modern Upasana

Upasana in Sanskrit means "sitting near." Traditionally, it refers to sitting near a symbol of the Divine–fire, a deity, or a teacher. Our gadgets glow like mini fires, yet they seldom kindle reverence. I decided to repurpose one device into a sacred ally. At sunset, I open the music app on my phone and play a twelve-minute *Lalitha Sahasranamam* on Spotify. Then I put the phone face-down and light a clay lamp beside it. The chant ends, the screen remains dark, the lamp flickers. For those twelve minutes, I do nothing else. The ritual marks the hinge between the workday and evening.

My cousin, Bulbul, initially teased me: "Our phone is doing aarti to itself." But she admits the house feels gentler afterward. The dog stops pacing. Even the neighbour's television seems to lower its volume, though that may be our perception adjusting.

Such re-ritualization is less about piety and more about neural patterning. *The brain loves cues.*

When we pair device usage with intentional pauses, the limbic hunger re-wires. Gradually, the very sight of a locked screen can remind us to pause, like Pavlov's bell inverted toward stillness.

Conclusion: The Pulse Behind the Screen

Presence is not the enemy of progress– it is the soil out of which meaningful progress sprouts. The Rig Veda teaches cosmic rhythm. When we align, action flows like Ganga's current, strong yet effortless. When we scroll compulsively, we paddle against the current, tiring the soul.

My thirty-day experiment did not make me a sage. I still get hooked by breaking news, still binge on cricket highlights. But each time the storm swells, I recall the silent dawn, the tanpura's hum, Saanvi's Marwa pouring like molten copper.

I remember that within every glowing rectangle beats a human pulse longing to feel fully alive.

In the next chapter we will explore what happens when that pulse collides with uncertainty, how faith can outshine fear. For now, as we lay this book down, resist the reflex to unlock your phone.

Sit back, notice the tingling in your fingertips, the hush beneath the traffic, the simple grace of being here–awake, without needing to become a pixel in someone else's feed. That single breath of unclaimed attention may be the most radical act of transcendence we can offer the digital age.

Chapter 6

Faith Over Fear: Trusting What We Can't Control

The Moment the Signal Dropped

In the last chapter, we pressed the pause button on our buzzing gadgets and tasted what presence feels like in a digital age. Some of my friends who read the first draft wrote to me that this book helped us try digital-detoxing. We deleted three apps and then, almost instinctively, reached for them again. It was awkward, we confessed, to sit in that gap between the old reflex and the new intention. That gap is exactly where today's exploration begins, because the gap is full of unknown: What will happen to my work, my friendships, my relevance if I step away? The mind whispers worst-case scenarios. That whisper is fear.

I want to introduce you all to Prerana, a marketing executive from Pune who joined one of my retreats in the Western Ghats. On the first evening, we collected everyone's phones. We did this gently, with velvet pouches and numbered tags like a valet service for gadgets. Prerana handed hers over but lingered at the table as though she had just surrendered an oxygen tank. "My clients will kill me," she said with a nervous laugh. Then, softer, "I don't trust that things will be okay if I'm not watching." That sentence could have been etched on every worried forehead in the room. It is the anthem of our times–I don't trust that things will be okay unless I control them.

And still, the human heart has been chanting a different refrain for millennia–sab kuchh tera (nothing is mine to control).

Geeta calls it *Isvara-arpana,* offering the fruits of action back to the source. How do we reconcile these two refrains–modern controls and ancient surrender–inside a single nervous system?

That is the pilgrimage of this chapter.

The Quiet Argument Between Two Brains

Neuroscientists speak of the limbic system, the part of the brain that scans for danger and pumps in cortisol. The ancients had their own map. In Kathopanishad, the worried mind is compared to a charioteer gripping the reins too tightly, whipping the horses of the senses. The chariot wobbles; the ride becomes jerky. Meanwhile, a deeper intelligence–the atman–sits in the back seat, serene and untouched. Modern MRI machines and ancient Sanskrit verses point to the same tug-of-war: one part of us is built to predict and dominate while the other part is built to witness and trust.

When we hear the word faith, perhaps we picture incense or pews,or childhood prayers that felt compulsory. Forget those images for a moment.

Faith, in the spiritual vocabulary we are exploring, is a neuro-emotional skill–the ability to rest attention in the back seat instead of forever grabbing the reins.

It is not blind belief; it is courageous relaxation.

The Farmer Who Smiled at the Clouds

Let me take you away from the corporate corridors to a village called Jevra-Sirsa in Chhattisgarh where we farmed napier and barseen. Monsoons can be fickle, and that year the clouds refused to burst.

Borewells and ponds dried; gossip flourished. Everyone fretted except old Rajinder, a lean man with silver stubble who owned one of the smaller plots. He still rose before dawn, tilled, cleared weeds, hummed Kabir couplets. My uncle mocked him one evening–"Why waste energy? The crop is doomed." Rajinder shrugged and pointed his chin at the horizon. "Baadal ka kaam hai barasna," he said. "The clouds will do their work. A farmer's dharma is to keep the field ready."

I remember this vividly because, as kids, we secretly wanted the fields to fail–a drought meant we could skip school to help families fetch water. But two weeks later a late monsoon thundered across the sky. Rajinder's land soaked up the first gush–weeds did not overrun his furrows because he had tended them faithfully. Other plots were half cleared–their owners had surrendered to despair. Rajinder's harvest fed three villages. He told us later, half joking, that the gods reward those who meet them halfway. But really it was his everyday faith-work, guided by trust and not the forecast, that saved the season.

Some readers would bristle at such stories saying, "Fine for farmers, but not for all. Hindu cosmology describes the same principle with different imagery. The Puranas say Vishnu dreams worlds into being, Brahma shapes them, and Shiva dissolves them. Creation is cyclic, never static. Everything we touch is already in motion toward transformation. Which means that clenching harder is not mastery–it is delusion.

Real mastery is surfing the wave, knowing we will fall underwater, trusting that another wave will lift us. *Surfers call it flow; Geeta calls it yoga-sthiti, steady union.*

My Own Cliff Edge

Guys, I want to confess. I did not grow up serene. By twenty-seven I had insomnia, gastritis, and a talent for catastrophising. My mantra was "What if?" What if the visa is denied? What if my partner gets bored? What if this book flops? A mentor asked me to watch the mind like a wildlife documentary. I noticed the mind always sprinted ahead, canvassing future disasters. But these disasters were sketches, not reality. Ninety percent of them never materialised.

Then came the cliff edge. My friend suffered a sudden stroke. I flew home, sat in the ICU watching machines breathe for him, and realized I controlled nothing–not the neurons in his brain nor the next five minutes. The only power I had was presence– holding his warm but unresponsive hand, praying silently, surrendering outcomes. He survived, though partially paralyzed, and our family reorganised life around that new reality. Years later his mother said, "That stroke forced us to trust God more than our friend's plans." It sounded sentimental until I saw the data–medical bills met by unexpected insurance, therapy slots opening at the last minute, a cousin quitting his job abroad to help. The universe rallied when we stopped arguing with it.

Fear pretends to be rational, but often it is an ancient emotion wearing modern costumes.

In Rig Veda, scarcity was described as Vritrasura, a serpent that hoarded waters so crops could not grow. Indra slays the serpent, releasing rivers.

Symbolically, scarcity is overcome not by storing every drop but by breaking the illusion of hoarding. Indra's thunderbolt is essentially a liberation of flow.

When we cling, we become the serpent–when we trust, we become the river.

Breath as a Tether to the Eternal

Meditation teachers in India have a phrase: *Shwas ko Ishwar mano*, consider the breath divine.

Each inhale arrives unbidden; each exhale exits without negotiations. Breathing is the body's repetitive proof that letting go is the natural sequel of receiving.

Sit quietly and pay attention–we do not push carbon dioxide out with strategy meetings–the body releases effortlessly. If we hold breath in fear, the body fights back until we surrender.

The Buddha discovered this under a fig tree in Bodh Gaya, but so did countless rishis by the Narmada or in the Himalayan caves. The practice is simple, but not easy–trust the breath, ride it like a ferry over the turbulence of thought. When fear screams, "What if?" the breath whispers, "We are still afloat."

The Dance of Karma and Grace

One analysis of surrender to divinity is that it can breed passivity. But Indian scriptures present karma and grace as partners, not competitors. Karma is action aligned with dharma, our inner compass. Grace is the wind that fills the sails.

A sailor still ties knots, studies currents, and patches holes. But he also knows the wind is none of his doing.

Action without openness is arrogant–openness without action is inertia. The sweet spot is a cooperative dance.

In the Ramayana, Hanuman leaps across the ocean to Lanka. Before jumping, he bows to the sun, to the wind-god, to every teacher. His effort is colossal–he pushes mountains aside–but his faith fuels it. At one point the sea goddess rises, offering him rest. He declines, saying the mission cannot wait. That story lodged in my adolescent mind–true faith is not lying on a beach waiting for destiny–it is strategic, persistent, and yet light-hearted, because the outcome is surrendered.

Practical Micro-Surrenders

We might wonder how to translate mythic leaps into Monday mornings. The secret lies in micro-surrenders.

Every day offers dozens of moments to practice releasing the illusion of control. When the elevator stops at every floor and we are late, that is a divine curriculum. When our toddler spills turmeric milk on the only white shirt we own, that is a pop quiz. Each incident is a mini-Geeta scene: we can grip, or we can breathe.

I used to rehearse conversations in my head before important events, sculpting perfect sentences. But people rarely follow the script. Nowadays, I write bullet points of intent, then let dialogue unfold. I cannot count how many gatherings have bloomed because I listened instead of forcing my lines.

Faith gives curiosity the space to work. Fear is tyrannical; it wants only predetermined outcomes.

Ishvara Pranidhana [Samarpan to Divine] in the Yoga Sutras

Patanjali, in his Yoga Sutras, lists surrender to the divine, *Ishvara Pranidhana*, as a direct path to samadhi. When I first encountered that line, after joining The Art of Living and studying yoga, I glossed over it, preferring muscular discipline: breath counts, asana alignment, effort. Later I discovered that surrender is not the easy option; it is an advanced level. It demands ego bankruptcy. We can muscle our way through a headstand. We cannot muscle our way through humility.

Years earlier, while working as a professor of communication and the art of conversation, I met a student namedJeetesh. He arrived in class with superb strength but chronic shoulder pain, forcing his inversions. I asked him to skip headstands for a month and focus instead on supported bridges and gentle pranayama. He resisted, then finally relented. The pain subsided. More interestingly, his temper cooled.

"I still like achieving," he told me, "but I don't feel as brittle. I get now that the pose is a conversation, not a conquest."

That is surrender, hidden inside biomechanics.

When Trust Goes Missing

We must address betrayal. Some readers carry scars, a business partner embezzled funds, a spouse walked out, a pandemic slashed savings. How do we trust again? Hindu texts and scriptures do not sanitize betrayal. Duryodhana cheats at dice, Ravana kidnaps Sita, even the gods break promises. The takeaway is not naivety but resilience.

Krishna tells Arjuna that dharma must sometimes be protected with a sword. Boundaries are part of faith. Letting go is not letting people crush us.

The City Will Shake, The Center Need Not

Earthquakes, layoffs, and elections–storms keep coming. The Geeta does not promise a calm planet, it promises an anchored soul. Modern Delhi trembles every few years with mild quakes. Once, I asked friends there, Do you stop buying apartments? They laughed. They retrofit buildings, keep emergency kits, but life goes on. This spiritual trust is a seismic retrofitting of the psyche.

Fear may rattle walls, but the foundation holds.

The Daily Rite of Release

By now we might crave technique. Here is one I practice nightly, a prayer taught by my mother. Sit on our bed, lights off. Recall the day in reverse, last email sent, dinner tasted, afternoon sun on the windowsill. Watch images float. For each moment, whisper, "I release." If regret arises, say, "I forgive." If pride arises, say, "I offer." Let the mind empty like a farmer's basket after market day. Sleep becomes sacred surrender. In the morning, before grabbing the phone, place a hand on the heart. Breathe three times. Say, "I am available for what unfolds."

Over months we will notice a looseness in the jaw, a quieter rush hour in the skull.

We have journeyed from battlefield panic to midnight breathing, from drought fields to ICU corridors. Along the way, perhaps a sentence nudged our shoulder, a memory welled up, a clenched muscle eased. Hold that ease gently. The storm outside still swirls, but a lamp inside has been refueled with trust.

In the coming chapter we will see what is faith if not the art of meeting ordinary moments with extraordinary presence? Keep your bow lifted, your breath steady.

Stillness is about walking into the most mundane corners of your day.

Chapter 7

Finding Sacredness in Ordinary Life

The Quiet After Surrender

We closed the last chapter by letting go, by unclenching the mental fist that tries to control everything. When we loosen that grip, what remains is an unexpected quiet, something like the hush that settles over a field after a summer storm. In that hush, life is still entirely the same and yet somehow profoundly different. The dishes are still stacked beside the sink. E-mails still ping in the corner of our laptop. Children still shout from the next room. But the quality of attention we bring to these sights and sounds has changed.

Surrendering softens the edges.

It makes space for a different kind of seeing, a way of beholding the same familiar world and discovering that it is, in fact, a holy ground.

That is what this chapter is about. Not a new practice to add to our overflowing to-do list, but a new pair of eyes.

Elizabeth Barrett Browning once wrote, "Earth's crammed with heaven, and every common bush afire with God, but only he who sees takes off his shoes."

It shows how to recognize the fire in the bushes that line our daily commute, how to take off our shoes in the middle of a grocery aisle, how to bow if only inwardly before a sink full of bubbles. Because when the ordinary becomes the temple, stillness stops being a weekend retreat and starts being the air we breathe.

The Two Pilgrimages

I once met a corporate lawyer who visited India every December to meditate in the Himalayas. He would spend ten days in noble silence, drinking ginger tea, staring at snowcaps, and returning home with a calm that made his associates whisper about his "Buddha shield." Yet by March he confessed he was back to yelling at traffic and grinding his molars at night. "I need the mountain," he said, "Without it, I forget everything."

A few weeks later I met a single mother named Usha who hadn't left the city in years. What surprised me was how clear her gaze was, and how unhurried her speech was. She described waking before dawn, lighting a single candle in the living room, and sitting for ten minutes with her notebook open, not to brainstorm but to thank. Then she woke her daughter, made her breakfast, all while humming a lullaby from her own childhood. She told me that to her, the hiss of the kettle sounded like ocean surf. "I close my eyes and I'm at the beach," she giggled, stirring *upma*.

Two pilgrims, two very different itineraries. One travelled thousands of miles, the other travelled thousands of tiny moments. Which journey is harder? The lawyer saves up vacation time, books flights, and endures altitude sickness. Usha confronts the relentless ordinariness of socks and cereal and fluorescent office lights.

The truth is, both journeys demand courage.

But only one teaches us how to locate transcendence in the checkout line when the register jams and the couple in front of us is arguing about carbonated water flavours.

Only one prepares us for the real terrain of life, which is mostly plain, largely repetitive, occasionally heartbreaking, and laced with pockets of luminous grace.

The Three Secrets of the Sacred Ordinary

I want to offer you three secrets my teachers passed down. They are not steps or tips, because we cannot pull holiness out of a moment the way we yank an olive pit from its flesh. But if we hold these secrets patiently, they may sprout inside us like seeds under warm soil.

The first secret is attention without an agenda. Let our gaze rest on an object the way morning dew rests on a leaf, lightly, without wanting anything. If we stare at the leaf hoping for a spiritual high, we tighten. But if we look because looking is itself a form of love, we soften, and through that softness the sacred seeps.

The second secret is affection for imperfection. Our kitchen floor will have breadcrumbs. The city bus will smell like stale coffee. The voice on the other end of the phone will mispronounce our name. If we wait for conditions to be immaculate, we postpone heaven indefinitely.

The third secret is a willingness to be surprised. The wise never get old in spirit because they expect wonder to ambush them daily. They do not demand it, but they suspect it lurks around every corner. That suspicion keeps their eyes bright. Children do this naturally, while adults cultivate it intentionally. In Zen they speak of "beginner's mind."

Rumi puts it differently: "Sell your cleverness and buy bewilderment."

A Walk to the Corner Store

Let me show you how these secrets operate in the wild.

Not long ago, I set out to buy milk. My phone was in my pocket, buzzing every few minutes with group-chat jokes and headline alerts. I resisted the urge to scroll and instead decided to test my beginner's eye. The sidewalk was cracked, weeds tilting through the fissures. I bent to touch one purplish rose flower and felt its velvet underside. A lady in a blue cardigan waved at someone across the street, and I noticed how her cardigan matched the sky, exactly the same shade of unsent email blue. The bakery vent exhaled cinnamon. A skateboard clacked.

None of these facts are extraordinary, yet gathering them felt like dipping a toe into eternity. By the time I reached the store, I was steady in a way caffeine cannot replicate. I purchased milk, thanked the cashier sincerely, and walked home. Total elapsed time, nine minutes. No angels descended, no epiphanies unfurled. But the boundary between me and the world had thinned. I was breathing more than air, I was breathing belonging.

When Life Feels Too Raw

There will be mornings when the chai tastes like reheated sadness, when the inbox mocks us with subject lines we dread opening, when the very idea of finding sacredness in laundry feels absurd. On such days, remember that reverence does not mean pretending everything is rosy.

Sacredness is spacious enough to hold agony.

If we can manage nothing else, sit at the edge of our bed, place one hand on our chest, and say, "Even this." Even this pain is part of the dance. Even this fatigue is woven into the cosmic loom. We are not praising the hurt, we are acknowledging its place in the wider tapestry. The moment we do, we have already stepped into a larger room. That room is sacred ground.

The Science Sneaks Up

Some readers prefer data over poetry, so here it is. Research suggests that brief moments of wonder, what scientists call “awe experiences”, are linked to reduced inflammation and increased unselfishness.

MRI scans reveal that when subjects gaze at something vast or beautiful, the brain’s default mode network, the home of self-referential chatter, quiets and regions tied to empathy and collaboration light up. That means every time we pause to admire the pattern of rain on our windshield, we nudge our nervous system toward calm and our social impulses toward kindness. What the mystics framed as reverence, the neuroscientists now chart in colorful brain maps.

Different lenses, same truth–the ordinary can rewire us.

The Invisible Apprenticeship

We do not need to add anything new to our schedule to become an apprentice of the ordinary. We are already surrounded by teachers. The kettle is teaching patience, the traffic light is teaching trust, the shoelace is teaching intention. Each moment issues an invitation to kneel inwardly and whisper, “Teach me.” Sometimes the lesson will be pleasant. Sometimes it will scald. Either way, the curriculum is comprehensive, and graduation is ongoing.

One afternoon, exhausted after a string of Zoom calls, I slumped at my desk and noticed a spider rappelling from the ceiling. I could have swatted it reflexively. Instead, I watched. The spider dangled, swung gently in the draft from the air vent, then reeled itself back up. Down, up, down, up, as if testing the line’s tensile strength. It struck me that the spider was practicing resilience, rehearsing for the day a storm might tear its web. I realized I, too, was rehearsing resilience every time I sat through another glitchy meeting. The spider and I were colleagues. My fatigue softened into camaraderie. I returned to work oddly refreshed.

Before we close this chapter, I invite you to perform a tiny ceremony with me right now. It will hardly take sixty seconds. Wherever you are, pause reading for a moment and look around. Let our eyes land on the first object that catches them. It could be a pen, a coffee mug, a slice of afternoon sunlight on the wall. Resist the urge to label or judge it. Instead, trace its outline slowly with your gaze, the way a finger might trace the rim of a bowl. Notice texture, colour, shadow. Imagine that object as the last thing you will ever see.

Would you see it differently? Would the pen become a house of worship? Would the sunlight become a hymn?

Hold the gaze for two more beats. Then gently release.

What we just did is both nothing and everything. It is the same gesture my grandmother offered me with that soapy teacup. When repeated throughout the day, three seconds here, five seconds there, it reenchants reality. It deposits coins into a bank account of presence, interest compounded by gratitude.

We have wandered through bedrooms and bedside vigils, gathering proof that the sacred is a shameless eavesdropper, listening at every doorway of our life, waiting for permission to enter. We do not need to speak Sanskrit or light incense. We only need to widen the aperture of our attention and dare to be astonished by toast.

Yet, even as we cultivate this inner altar, a question presses forward. What about the moments when we're alone in a crowded city, scrolling through feeds that promise connection but often deliver emptiness? How do we translate our newfound reverence into actual relationships–a sense that we belong to something larger than our private bubble of wonder?

That's where we are heading next.

Loneliness is the slow pandemic of our age, and sacredness, like love, longs to be shared. Let's step into that conversation together.

Chapter 8

Loneliness and Connection: The Spiritual Bond

There's an Echo in the Room

When we finished exploring the surrender in the last chapter, I asked you to place a few of your fears on the palm of your hand and watch them drift away like paper boats on a river. Perhaps you felt lighter for a moment, you closed the book, glanced around, and noticed something else sitting beside you. It was an ache more delicate than fear and quieter than anxiety, but equally persistent.

Loneliness has that stealthy nature. It rarely announces itself with trumpets; it appears as a faint echo in an otherwise ordinary room, an echo we can't locate, yet can't ignore.

I felt that echo during the global lockdown of 2020. My apartment was filled with devices, phone, laptop, and speakers - all pinging and blinking, clamouring to entertain me. A hundred conversations were technically available at the swipe of a finger, yet the silence between those beeps felt bigger. One night, while waiting for sourdough to rise, during that collective bread-baking mania, I realized I had spoken out loud exactly twice that day, once to share my grocery PIN with the delivery person and second, to apologize to my plant for forgetting to water it. The dough rose, the notifications multiplied, and still the apartment felt like outer space.

We know this feeling. Maybe it visits us during the slow drip of a Sunday afternoon, or in the middle of a crowded subway when everyone stares at screens. Maybe it tiptoes in after an evening of scrolling through parties we weren't invited to, vacations we can't afford, lovers we haven't met.

Loneliness, paradoxically, is amplified by what our era promises will connect us.

Wires Without Warmth

Sociologists call this the "loneliness paradox". We are the most connected generation in history, and yet, surveys show record levels of perceived isolation. We might Facetime a friend in Dubai, binge a dating app carousel of charming strangers, attend a virtual yoga class in Bali, and still crawl into bed feeling like an astronaut lost between galaxies. Why?

Partly because the connection has two faces. One is informational, the exchange of words, photos, emoticons, and data. The other is relational, the feeling of being witnessed, understood, and held in mutual presence. Digital platforms excel at the first face and often bypass the second. You can send me ten heart-eye emoticons, but unless I feel your actual heart meeting mine in the messy, unscripted aliveness of real time, the warmth doesn't quite permeate.

Neuroscience gives us language to match that intuition. Human eyes evolved to detect microexpressions only within four feet of another face. Oxytocin, the neurotransmitter of trust, surges when we hear the subtle tremor in a loved one's voice or feel the warmth of their hand. No bandwidth, however broadband, can fully transmit those micro-signals. So the nervous system obeys biology, not marketing copy; it registers a shortfall. That shortfall is what whispers, I'm alone, even as our inbox glows with new messages.

The Yogic View of One Heart

Long before fiber-optic cable, sages from many traditions diagnosed the core illusion that spawns loneliness, the idea of separateness. The Upanishads call it avidya: ignorance of our underlying unity. Buddhism describes it as the false "I" that imagines itself cut off from the web of life.

Christian mystics speak of the fragmented self that has forgotten it lives in God.

Different languages, same understanding. The borders we draw around identity are provisional at best and hallucinatory at worst.

In yogic philosophy, consciousness is compared to a crystal prism. When pure light passes through the prism, it appears as many colours, yet the light itself remains singular.

We, the colours, forget the prism and begin arguing about shades. Loneliness, from this vantage, is the sorrow of being a blue-ray, convinced it has been expelled from the spectrum.

If that sounds poetic but abstract, let me offer a concrete experiment. The next time you sit quietly, close your eyes and notice the flow of breath. Follow it in, follow it out. After a minute, imagine the air in our lungs originating from the trees outside our window. Carbon dioxide we exhaled yesterday is currently feeding a maple leaf that will exhale oxygen for us tomorrow. Keep tracing the exchange, leaf to lung, lung to leaf, organisms passing invisible gifts. Where does the tree end and we begin? The intellect says, "That's a tree, this is me." The body, inhaling its partner's exhale, remembers otherwise. In that remembered unity, loneliness softens.

From Isolation to Intimacy

Knowing we are interwoven is one thing, feeling it through experience is another. During the second year of the pandemic, I joined a neighbourhood mutual-aid group. Our first project was delivering groceries to seniors who were sheltering in place. I was assigned to Mrs. Banerjee, an eighty-three-year-old widow with arthritis and a fondness for mango pickle. Every Friday I wheeled a cart to her apartment, left the bags at her door, rang the bell, and stepped back six feet. She would appear in her sari, hands pressed together in greeting, eyes gleaming behind foggy glasses.

For months our exchange was wordless, masked, yet magnetic. One afternoon she invited me to keep the change. I declined. She insisted. I declined again. Exasperated, she blurted, "Beta, let me feel useful!" Something in that sentence cracked my heart open. I realized the deliveries weren't merely assistance, they were threads stitching two isolated lives into a small but radiant tapestry.

Loneliness loosened its grip, not because we shared perfect conversation, but because we allowed ourselves to belong to each other.

The Miracle of Showing Up

A mentor once told me that the most spiritual sentence in any language is "I'm here."

Presence, offered sincerely, radiates healing at higher frequencies than a library of sacred texts. When someone sits with us in grief without trying to fix it, when a friend remembers our favourite snack and slides it across the table after a long day, when a stranger meets our eyes on the train and nods as if to say, I recognize your humanity; these moments stitch the torn fabric of the world.

Over a few months, during my retreats, I saw participants arrive burdened by chronic loneliness. What transforms them is not mere lectures on non-duality, it's the alchemy in the dining hall when they share stories over soup. During one retreat, a software engineer, Akshat, confessed he felt invisible at work and numb at home. Another participant, Meghna, an elementary school teacher, said she felt smothered by too much social input from children yet lonely at night. By day three, Akshat and Meghna were inseparable, spotted walking the forest path in deep conversation. I asked what clicked. Akshat said, "She listened like every word mattered." Meghna added, "He let me be silent when I needed to." They gave each other precisely what they needed, but only because they first risked exposing their emptiness.

Here's what that reveals, community is not a place we join, it's an energy we generate by showing up authentically. We might live in the same apartment block for ten years without community, or we might ignite it in a single evening simply by daring to say, "Hi, I'm new here, and I'd love to help with the dishes." Spiritual masters didn't build followings through charisma alone, they cooked meals, tended wounds, swept floors. Their presence said, "I'm with you," long before their sermons elaborated on oneness.

The Thread We Hold

Before we pivot to the power of daily rituals in the next chapter, I invite you to test something simple over the coming week. The experiment requires no list, no app, and no complicated protocol, just the intention and presence. Each morning, as soon as you notice the first urge to check our phone, pause. Place a hand on your chest, breathe, and silently ask, "Who might need my presence today?" Wait for a name or face to arise. Then reach out to that person before the day sweeps you into its riptide. It could be a voice note, a handwritten postcard, a visit to share leftover soup. The form is irrelevant, sincerity is everything.

When we do this, we transform the phantom ache of loneliness into a bridge of connection.

Neuroscience will confirm oxytocin levels rise. Spiritual texts will say we remembered the prism. Our own heart will feel warmer, fuller, and steadier in the storm. And when the night falls, instead of scrolling for proof that we belong, we will already know that the bond is not abstract but a live thread, and we hold one end in our hand.

That thread grows stronger when it is woven into daily rhythms, small, sacred gestures performed not intermittently but as reliably as sunrise. Rituals, as we will see next, are the scaffolding for the soul, giving shape to the indefinable longing we have been tracing here. In the pages ahead, we will learn how to build that scaffolding together. For now, close our eyes, whisper "I'm here," and feel the room answer back, So am I.

Chapter 9

The Power of Daily Rituals

The Invisible Architecture of Our Days

Pause for a moment and run your mind over the last twenty-four hours. You'll probably remember the big things first: work, commute, maybe a workout, maybe that late-night scrolling session you promised ourselves you'd avoid. But look closer and you'll notice countless small moves you repeat almost without thinking– the way you cradle the coffee mug in your palms, the phrases you murmur when you lock the front door, the brief self-grooming before joining a video call. These microscopically ordinary gestures are our rituals, whether or not we have ever called them that.

Ritual is simply repeated activity infused with meaning.

The meaning can be intentional or accidental, conscious or inherited, nourishing or depleting. A doom-scroll at midnight is as much a ritual as lighting a candle at dawn. The difference is that only one of these two is likely to deliver us back to ourselves.

During the past eight chapters we have explored slowness, presence, surrender, and sacredness. All of those ideas hover a few inches above the ground until ritual nails them into the soil of daily life.

Ritual is the invisible architecture that turns inspiration into incarnation.

It is how stillness grows legs and learns to walk with you wherever you go: the supermarket, the classroom, the board meeting, and the hospital waiting room.

If the modern storm is in constant motion, ritual is the lighthouse that flashes at the same frequency no matter how wild the waves become.

Now, we will step inside that lighthouse and study the machinery, and then build a small beacon of our own.

Why the Mind Craves Repetition

Neuroscientists often describe the brain as a pattern-recognition machine. What looks to us like personality is often the brain's fierce preference for the familiar. A familiar pathway costs less energy, an unfamiliar one demands glucose, oxygen, vigilance, and the willingness to risk embarrassment. This is why we can reach for our phone on the nightstand before we are fully awake, yet struggle mightily to begin a morning meditation. One path is grooved, the other is fresh snow.

Ancient mystics recognised this principle long before MRI scanners lit up our headlines. They knew that if we braided intentionality into a repeated act, the act would eventually unfold almost automatically, carrying our intention like a scent in the air. The Sanskrit word samskara describes both a rite of passage and an impression etched on the mind. Modern psychology echoes the same insight with the phrase, "neurons that fire together wire together."

That is why ritual is not spiritual window dressing. It is the neurobiological conveyor belt that lifts an insight out of the realm of ideas and drops it into the rhythm of heartbeat and breath. Insight without ritual is a seed left on a windowsill, beautiful, but unlikely to sprout roots.

From Temple to Kitchen

For many of us the word ritual conjures images of incense, garments, and chanting monks. Those ceremonies are beautiful, yet the heart of ritual is independent of place or costume. I learned this from my mother, a woman who never once used the word mindfulness, and yet embodied it better than any influencer I follow.

Every morning at five, she would stand in her little kitchen, close her eyes, and touch her fingertips to her forehead, her lips, and her heart. Then she would strike a match, light the stove, and whisper a line that translates roughly as "May this flame feed all who are hungry."

The gesture took ten seconds. The meal she cooked took much longer and fed not only the family but also the stray dog that waited outside the back door.

I once asked her why she bothered with the whispered words. She shrugged and said, "If I remember that the fire is sacred, the whole morning goes better."

There was no divinity, no talk, only a subtle shift in loyalty from autopilot to awareness. That shift was contagious; even as a child I felt calmer when I entered that kitchen, as if the walls themselves were slightly more awake than walls normally are.

The Rituals We Inherit, the Rituals We Create

Not every ritual serves us. My friend Leila grew up in a household where Sunday mornings were reserved for a three-hour temple service followed by an equally rigid lunch where every plate had to be spotless. As an adult, she avoided anything that resembled a ritual. When burnout knocked her last year, she reluctantly tried the most basic of practices–sitting on her bedroom floor at 7:00 a.m. with a mug of tea and three conscious breaths. The first week felt silly. The second week felt bearable. By the third week she realised she was no longer scrolling headlines before her feet hit the floor.

Leila is now the unlikely curator of morning "tea-time" that gathers half a dozen exhausted parents on Zoom call, cameras off, microphones muted, and each holding a warm cup, while a bell rings once to begin and once to end. Ten minutes, no doctrine, only shared presence. She still won't call it a ritual in public, but her nervous system recognises it as one.

This is the subtle alchemy we all possess–the power to sift inherited rituals, keep the gold, melt the lead, and mint new coins for the next generation. We do not have to be a monk or a mystic or a yoga teacher.

We only need to decide that something we do every day deserves to be done consciously.

Designing a Ritual That Fits Our Life

By now you might be wondering, 'But how do I choose?'

With so many options, journaling, chanting, stretching, cold plunging, and gratitude lists, how do I avoid turning ritual into yet another item on the self-improvement conveyor belt?

The answer is startlingly simple: Start where your attention already wants to go, then wrap it in awareness. If you love coffee, let the grinding of beans become a bell of mindfulness. If you love running, bow to your shoes and whisper a line of gratitude for your legs before you lace up. If you love music, press play on the same song at the same time each night. Or just close your eyes, and let the first three breaths wash the day away.

What makes a ritual effective is not its exotic flair but its consistency and the quality of presence we bring. My friend Sudesh begins every Zoom meeting by silently saying the phrase "Only love is real" as he clicks the unmute button. No one on the call has any idea, but over time his colleagues have noticed that Sudesh's voice is the calmest in a crisis. That single silent sentence is a tuning fork, it brings his mind back to a key that resonates with trust rather than fear.

Let me share my own. Each evening I open the same thin book of poetry, sometimes Ghalib, sometimes

Khusrau or Bulle Shah, and let my finger land on a random page. I read one stanza aloud. Then I close the book, turn off the lamp, and place both palms on the wooden desktop. Five breaths, eyes closed. On the inhale I think of receiving. On the exhale I think of releasing. The whole affair lasts less than two minutes, yet I have noticed that when I skip it, my dreams grow jagged and when I keep up with it, sleep becomes a velvet hallway into dawn.

Is this magic? No. It is neurochemistry. But neurochemistry can feel like magic when we ride it skillfully.

When Rituals Break

Of course, even the most dearly held ritual will occasionally shatter. A newborn cries, a flight is delayed, a pandemic rearranges the calendar. Some days you will find yourself brushing your teeth in the bathroom of a petrol pump station, scrolling headlines, hating the universe. That is okay.

Ritual is not a performance for cosmic approval. It is an anchor.

I learned this the hard way during my mother's illness. For months, my days were swallowed by hospital corridors and insurance phone calls. My beloved morning meditation shrank to thirty seconds in the elevator. I would stand very still, watch the floor numbers blink, and whisper, "Here. Now. Thank you." That was all. Did it erase the fear? No. But it punched a pinhole in the darkness, and sometimes a pinhole is enough to keep breathing.

Collective Ritual: Why Do We Need Each Other?

So far, we have focused on solitary practices. But human beings are tribal creatures. A ritual performed alone is a seed, a ritual performed together is a forest.

Remember the early days of the pandemic when people leaned out of apartment windows to applaud healthcare workers each evening. For two minutes, strangers became a choir. In my neighbourhood the applause soon evolved. Someone added a harmonica, another banged a pot, children waved flashlights in the dusk. That brief nightly ceremony did not shorten the infection curve, but it softened our collective terror. We went to bed knowing our voices could still combine into something larger than despair.

This principle is why weddings, funerals, graduations, and sports championships feel charged with electricity.

The choreography of a shared ritual braids individual nervous systems into a single field. Scientists call the phenomenon limbic resonance and the mystics call it communion. Either way, it heals.

If we feel chronically lonely, find or create a ritual that requires at least one witness. Meet a friend for a silent sunrise, light a candle before our weekly book club, and agree to a one-minute gratitude swap with our partner before falling asleep. Ritual is love wearing work clothes.

The Danger of Ritual Without Spirit

Every medicine has a shadow side. Rituals can become robotic. The mind loves to hijack a good thing and strip it for parts. We have seen this happen in institutions that recite prayers while ignoring the poor, corporations that hold diversity pledges without changing hiring practices, families that say grace and then fight over dessert.

The antidote is not to discard ritual but to return to its living core. A single breath taken with sincere attention restores the inner pulse.

Vietnamese Monk and peace activist, Thich Nhat Hanh, used to tell his students, "The practice is to practice."

In other words, the point of bowing is not the bow but the awareness that flowers within the bow. When awareness vanishes, ritual may still carry cultural value, but its power to liberate the heart evaporates.

I remind myself of this each New Year's Day when I sit down with an elaborate vision-board template. The first twenty minutes feel inspired- the next twenty often devolve into frantic scribbles about something else. When that happens, I close the laptop, stand up, and stretch. The body never lies-if the shoulders are clenched, the ritual has drifted off course. At that point the most spiritual thing I can do is pour a glass of water, step onto the balcony, and watch the sky.

When the World Ends and Begins Again

I once attended the cremation ceremony of a relative in my hometown. Many people gathered in a silent procession. In that breathtaking moment I realised that ritual is humanity's way of telling time on a cosmic scale. Birth, death, sunrise, and eclipse, these thresholds are too vast for intellect alone. We need fire, song, incense, and synchronized breath to comprehend them in our bones.

The modern world rarely pauses long enough to mark such thresholds. We rush from Zoom call to headline to grocery line, forgetting that every day is a miniature birth and death. Morning kills the night, dusk buries the afternoon. Ritual reminds us to bow at each funeral and each initiation, to feel the hinge swing and know we are alive.

The pandemic, for all its cruelty, exposed our hunger for such markers. Weddings shrank to backyard vows, funerals were livestreamed to grieving screens, and yet we improvised, drive-through graduations, balcony concerts, masked tea ceremonies in city parks. We learned that ritual is less about the settings and more about presence.

A Twelve-Breath Practice to Anchor the Day

I would like to leave you with a practice that has carried me through airports, hospital rooms, and sleepless hotel nights. It requires no props, no mat, no app. Only twelve breaths, divided into four groups of three. I learned it from an elderly teacher who called it the "Compass." He said that no matter where we are, twelve conscious breaths will point us back to the True North.

In the first three breaths, notice the body. Feel the weight of gravity, the texture of clothing, the temperature of air against skin.

Second three breaths: notice sound. Let every hum, beep, bird-call, and heartbeat enter without judgment.

Third three breaths: notice thought. Watch each thought arise and dissolve like ink swirls in water. No need to change or improve them.

Final three breaths: return to intention. On each inhale silently ask, "What matters now?" On each exhale, let go of whatever does not.

That is all. Twelve breaths; around one minute. If we weave this minute into the hinges of dawn, noon, and dusk, we will have built a ritual that spans the day with only three minutes of clock time. Yet those minutes will infuse the remaining 1,437 with a subtler light.

Bringing It Home

We are nearly at the end of our journey together. Stillness is no longer a distant mountain but a small lamp we can carry in our palm.

Daily ritual is the oil that keeps the lamp burning.

In the closing chapter we will gather everything, slowness, presence, surrender, faith, and the quiet power of repeated acts, into a single realization, we are not merely the storm-tossed traveler, we are also the sky beneath the storm, vast and untroubled.

But before we step into that final space, pause. Listen. Perhaps choose one gesture right now, a fingertip to the heart, a whispered thank you, a slow sip of water, and let it mark this moment as sacred.

Feel the hinge swing. The door to the last chapter is already opening.

Chapter 10

Becoming the Stillness

The Wake Before Dawn

I want to begin with a confession. Last year in December, very early in the morning, I woke up in the dark, stepped onto the balcony outside my apartment, and did absolutely nothing for ten minutes. No breathing technique, no mantra, no posture checklist, just stood there in a threadbare sweater, listening.

At first all I heard was the buzz of fluorescent streetlamps and the low growl of the city's garbage trucks. But every day, minute by minute, the hum behind the hum grew louder until it felt as though the whole sky was inhaling with me. It was not that the world became quieter, it was that I finally let myself dissolve into its already-existing stillness.

This chapter is an invitation for you to do the same, not by mimicking my balcony ritual but by stepping into the living silence that is waiting beneath every gesture, word, and thought. By now we have practiced slowing down, digital fasting, surrender, mindful chores, honest conversation, and evening rituals. We have walked the bridge from hushed doings to sacred beings.

Now, we will cross the final bridge–recognising that stillness is not something we visit–it is what we are made of. The storm may still swirl, but we are about to discover the unmovable eye at its centre.

The Mirage of Arrival

Many of my friends and a few colleagues wrote and called me and said, "I feel calmer, but life keeps throwing curveballs. When will I finally arrive at perpetual peace?"

They picture a mountaintop where thoughts never intrude and traffic never honks. Let's puncture that mirage right here.

The goal is not to create a life of zero stimulus, the goal is to become a human being for whom stimulus no longer dictates the inner climate.

Imagine the ocean on a windy afternoon. Waves slap the shore in hectic succession, yet a few metres below, the water is steady as glass. A surfer falls headfirst, churns in the foam, and surfaces laughing because she knows the turbulence is thin. Likewise, the practices we have collected are surfboards, they give us balance on the surface so we can remember the depth beneath.

The moment we believe peace is an external destination, we hand our power to circumstances. The moment we realise peace is what remains when we stop outsourcing our attention, we have already arrived.

From Practice to Presence

Throughout the previous chapters, we used specific tools, breath counting, mindful eating, evening reflection. These are invaluable, but there comes a point where techniques must soften into second nature, the way training wheels lift from a child's bicycle once balance is learned. Otherwise, spirituality becomes another productivity hobby.

So how do we move from disciplined stillness to effortless stillness? *The answer is intimacy.*

The more intimately we witness what is happening right now, the hum of our laptop fan, the warmth in our palms, the echo of yesterday's conversation, the less grip the future and past have on us. Intimacy dissolves the imaginary distance between "me" and "experience," leaving only direct aliveness.

In that naked encounter, no technique is required, attention holds itself the way a mother naturally holds her newborn.

I invite you, my dear readers, to treat every technique as a doorway rather than a destination. Bow to it, walk through, then keep walking. When the need arises, we may return, but we will return with gentler steps, like a pilgrim who no longer prays for miracles because the ground beneath her feet is already holy.

I promised earlier that we would end with one simple practice, something so portable we cannot leave home without it.

Let us call it the Stillness Check-In. It takes less time than scrolling a social feed, costs nothing, and can be done anywhere, a bus seat, a bathroom stall, an elevator. Here is how it works.

First, when we notice the slightest hint of hurry or contraction, maybe our shoulders crawl toward our ears, our breath turns shallow, or our screen-tapping accelerates, pause. No moral judgment. Just pause as we would pause before stepping onto a stage. *Second*, feel the weight of gravity in our feet or hips, the raw contact with the ground or chair. Let the physical sensation anchor us in this single slice of time. *Third*, ask silently, "What is quieter than this?" Do not search for an answer, allow the question to widen our field of awareness the way night widens around a campfire.

In that widening, we will glimpse, or rather, be glimpsed by, the stillness that never left. Finally, proceed with our task, carrying the faint echo of quiet like a pebble in our pocket.

Practice this a dozen times a day, not as a chore but as a flirtation with the sacred. Soon you will discover that the check-in merges with living, the bell that rings us back to presence rings by itself, because it is us.

A Gift for the Road: The Ten-Day Integration Journey

Before we part ways, I want to offer you all a small gift, a condensed journey that braids together every insight we have explored.

For the next ten days, dedicate each sunrise to one chapter's theme.

Day one, observe the ancient whisper of restlessness. Day two, step out of the cult of doing. And so on, until day ten, when you circle back here, to stand as the quiet eye of the storm. No notebooks required, no rigid schedule. Simply wake, remember the day's seed, and let ordinary life water it. By sunset, jot down three sentences on how the seed sprouted. At the end of ten days you will possess not only knowledge, but lived memory, an internal scrapbook of stillness in motion.

Consider this your keepsake, slipped between the pages of the book like a pressed flower. Whenever chaos flares, open that memory and inhale its scent.

The Journey Continues in You

We have travelled from the storm's roar to its hushed centre. We have seen that stillness is not escape but engagement, not retreat but return. The practices, the stories, the science, all are fingers pointing to the same moon. Now close the book for a moment, feel the quiet pulse behind our ribs, and notice how the moonlight is already spilling across our own skin.

May your days be busy if they must, but never again noisy in the places that matter.

May your mind be clear water in which even suffering can see its reflection and soften.

The storm may continue outside these pages, yet inside us the sky is wide, the ocean deep, the stillness unbroken.

Take it with you. Become it.

And when someone next to you forgets, let your quiet resonate:

I bow to the stillness that you are.

And… this is not the end. It is the beginning.